MIDWINTERBLOOD

Also by Marcus Sedgwick

Blood Red, Snow White
The Book of Dead Days
The Dark Flight Down
The Dark Horse
Floodland
The Foreshadowing
The Kiss of Death
My Swordhand is Singing
Revolver
White Crow
Witch Hill

And for younger readers

The Raven Mysteries:
Flood and Fang
Ghosts and Gadgets
Lunatics and Luck
Vampires and Volts
Magic and Mayhem
Diamonds and Doom

For more information visit –
www.marcussedgwick.com
www.ravenmysteries.co.uk

MIDWINTERBLOOD

Marcus Sedgwick

Indigo

First published in Great Britain in 2011
by Indigo
a division of the Orion Publishing Group Ltd
Orion House
5 Upper St Martin's Lane
London WC2H 9EA
A Hachette UK Company

1 3 5 7 9 10 8 6 4 2

Hardback ISBN 978 1 78062 009 1
Trade paperback ISBN 978 1 78062 123 4

Printed in Great Britain by
Clays Ltd, St Ives plc

The Orion Publishing Group's policy is to use papers that are natural, renewable
and recyclable products made from wood grown in sustainable forests.
The logging and manufacturing processes are expected to conform to the
environmental regulations of the country of origin.

www.orionbooks.co.uk

For Maureen

Contents

PART ONE

Midsummer Sun

———

June 2073 – The Flower Moon

ട

One

———

The sun does not go down.

This is the first thing that Eric Seven notices about Blessed Island. There will be many other strange things that he will notice, before the forgetting takes hold of him, but that will come later.

For now, he checks his watch as he stands at the top of the island's solitary hill, gazing to where the sun should set. It has gone midnight, but the sun still shines, barely dipping its heavy rim into the sea on the far horizon.

The island is so far north.

He shakes his head.

He's thinking about Merle. How something seems to wait in her eyes. How he felt calm, just standing next to her.

'Well, so it is,' he says, smiling with wonder.

He's tired. His journey has been a long one.

The strangeness began on the plane.

The flight to Skarpness was not full, maybe half the seats were empty, but there was nevertheless a good number of people. Mining company folk mostly, heading to the northern interior, Eric guessed.

He took his seat by the window and did what everyone does before the instruction to switch off communications; he selected OneDegree on his device, and bumped.

And then . . . nothing.

He rebooted the app, and bumped again.

Nothing.

He shook his head, unable to understand it.

The OneDegree app is based on the principle of six degrees of separation. Eric knows all about it. As a journalist, it is his job to know about communication in its many forms. Since its invention, when some clever soul realised that it often takes not *six*, but merely *one* step to connect you to most other people in the world, the app, or its current version, sits in the palm of everyone's hand. When going on a journey, or arriving in a new place, the easiest way to make friends quickly is to bump the air around you with OneDegree. Maybe no one you know is on the same plane, but someone who knows someone you know is likely to be. Or someone who went to school with a friend of yours. Or who works where you worked ten years ago. And so on and so on. Then you have someone to pass the journey with, at the least, and maybe a new friend for life. And although that's never happened to Eric, in all his years of using OneDegree on so many solitary journeys around the world, he has never failed to find some kind of link among a group of a hundred or more who would otherwise have remained total strangers.

So that is why he stared a moment longer at his device, wondering if the new version had a bug.

4

As if something sinister had happened, he leaned out of his seat and a little furtively studied his fellow passengers.

They were a tough lot.

Miners, he thought. Tough.

Work and worry were drawn on their faces, in skin aged by the cold. They were silent, merely nodding at the smiling attendants who floated down the aisle, proffering drinks.

'You'll have to switch that off now, Mr Seven,' said a voice, and he turned to see one of them looking down at him. She checked her device, making sure she'd got his name right.

He scratched the back of his head, pushed a badly behaved strand of dark brown hair out of his eyes.

'Yes. Sorry, right. Only . . .'

He looked at his device.

'Yes, Mr Seven?'

He shook his head. How could he have managed not to bump anyone on the flight? Not even at the weakest level of connection.

'Nothing.'

The attendant smiled.

'Very good. Have a nice flight, Mr Seven.'

He did have a nice flight.

The plane arrowed due north, clinging to the coast almost the whole way. It was spectacularly beautiful.

The coastline was a broken fractal, the sea was deep

blue, the rocks of the shore gentle mottled greys and browns. Inland, the ground climbed steadily into forests, which eventually gave way to treeless mountaintops.

About noon the plane landed at Skarpness, and as Eric predicted, most of the passengers picked up transport heading for the big mine.

For the hundredth time, he pulled out the instructions the desk editor's assistant had given him, and made his way on foot to the ferry terminal, where he boarded the steam-boat for the short trip to Blessed Island.

He knows little about the place.

Just the rumours. But then, that's all anyone knows, and that, after all, is the whole point of his trip, to find out something about the island.

There is nothing much about it on the net. Nothing beyond the times of the steam-boat, the hours of sun-fall and moon-up, a brief history of the old fishing trade, now gone.

As for the rumours . . .

No first-hand accounts, no original source material. The pages that do mention them are simply rehashes of each other, leaving very few original hits to glean anything from.

So little to be read on the net; that's another strange thing about the place.

All he's heard are the rumours, stories, the speculation, and the swiftly lost words of whispered secrets, about the island where people have started to live forever.

Two

E ric Seven does not believe in love at first sight.
He corrects himself.

Even in that moment, the moment that it happens, he feels his journalist's brain make a correction, rubbing out a long-held belief, writing a new one in its place.

He did not believe in love at first sight. He thinks he might do now.

'I'm Merle,' she says. Her light hair falls across one eye as she shakes his hand, she flicks it aside. And smiles.

'Of course you are,' he says. Inside, he makes a note to punish himself later for such a lame reply, and yet, he had not said it with arrogance, or even an attempt at being funny. He said it as if someone else was saying it for him.

He was standing on the quayside, his single large backpack by his feet. Behind him, the steam-boat pulled away, heading back to the mainland. The few other passengers have already disappeared, vanishing into the narrow lanes of the island.

Everything is quiet.

The young woman called Merle half turns and gestures and now Eric notices a small group of people with her. They smile at him too.

One of them, an old man, steps forward.

'I'm Tor,' he says, and holds out his hand.

Eric shakes it, feeling a little uneasy again.

'How did you know I was coming?' he asks.

'Well, we didn't,' Tor says. 'But we don't get many visitors. Word of your arrival reached us, and we have come to meet you, Mr . . . Seven?'

'Yes. Yes, that's right. Eric Seven.'

Tor raises a whiskery eyebrow. His face is long and so weather-beaten it is hard to guess how old he is, and Eric notices that there is something wrong with one of his eyes. It's milky, and doesn't seem to focus. Maybe he's even blind in that eye. Eric tries not to stare.

'Well, so it is,' he says under his breath.

'Seven?' asks Tor. 'One of the True Modern Church?'

Eric shakes his head.

'My parents were. They were first generation converts, back in the twenty-twenties. I . . .' He stops, wonders what to say. 'I disappointed them. It means nothing to me.'

'So why keep the name?' Tor smiles. 'If I may ask.'

Eric pauses.

'Many reasons, I suppose. Respect, perhaps. And although I'm not religious, I do like the idea that the renaming represents.'

Merle, who's been watching this exchange, tilts her head, just a fraction more. Her hair falls across her eyes again. Eric notices it, and feels himself fall even faster for her. He feels ridiculous. He's wondering what to say, what to do, but she's asking him something.

'What's that?' she asks. 'The idea behind it?'

'The founders of the True Modern Church had many

strongly held principles and beliefs, but much of their teaching is more practical, to do with how people relate to each other, to society and so on. They believed that names were shackles, and badges, and that they were full of meaning, and history, and were therefore weapons of prejudice and of snobbery. Anyone who joins the Church is invited to select a new name, one without meaning, without history, without prejudice. Numbers are common in the Church; they seemed neutral. Devoid of meaning.'

Merle tilts her head some more. Eric wants to shout with joy, and pictures himself throwing his arms round her. He does neither, but wonders what it would feel like to touch her.

'But Mr Seven,' Tor says, 'All words have meaning. Especially names. Even new ones. And as for numbers . . .'

Eric shrugs again.

'What was your parents' name before they joined the Church?'

Eric is thrown, as he realises that he doesn't want to talk about his parents. He changes the subject. He looks at Tor and Merle, and the two women and another man who are with them. They are all smiling at him.

'So, are you always this friendly to visitors?'

'We don't get many visitors,' Tor repeats.

Eric notices that his question has not been answered directly, but lets it drop.

'And why have you come to Blessed Island?' Tor continues.

He smiles, and just as Eric is about to tell him, something makes him stop short. But it's best not to lie, and in these circumstances he usually falls back on the simple method of giving just enough of the truth.

'I'm a journalist,' he explains. 'My editor wants a feature about your island. She's heard it's a beautiful place. A special place.'

Eric can already see that this much is true.

Behind the welcoming party, a little lane splits into two, one path running off around the shore line, the other up over a gentle rise. He can see modest, beautifully designed wooden houses, most painted in rich colours: deep reds, light blues, earthy yellows. They have small rose bushes and tall birches. Bees hum in the air.

Behind him the blue sea slaps at the stones of the quay and gulls cry overhead.

'And will you be staying long?' asks Tor, looking at Eric's single bag.

'I don't know yet,' Eric says.

He looks at Merle. She smiles.

Three

Eric Seven sat in the Cross House with Tor and the others who met him at the ferry. Except Merle.

'Where were you thinking of staying, Mr Seven?' Tor had asked, as they walked down the island, south from the quay.

'Please. Call me Eric.'

'Where were you thinking of staying, Eric?'

'I don't know.'

Tor smiled.

'We don't have a hotel. As I said, we . . .'

'Don't get many visitors,' Eric finished for him. 'But there must be some kind of guest house, perhaps?'

'No,' Tor had said. 'There is nothing of that sort. But don't worry. We will make some arrangements for you. In the meantime, you are welcome at my house. We can take tea while the arrangements are made.'

They'd walked along the narrow lane, called Homeway, gently curving from time to time, but always heading south down the island, with pretty gardens and sweet houses on either side, some right on the track, some set back on little rocky cliffs among the trees. Now and again, side roads head off; even smaller, twistier paths. The paths have tiny white-on-blue signs: The Bend, The Backbend, The Green, The Crook.

All very, very beautiful.

As they'd walked, Eric saw people sitting out at tables in their gardens, enjoying the evening sunshine, taking a glass of wine, or even supper. Everyone had waved and called to Tor, who'd nodded back, smiling.

After ten minutes they'd arrived at a crossroads, where Homeway crossed another track of the same size, called Crossway.

'My home,' Tor had said, indicating the largest house on the island that Eric had so far seen. Set back on a low hill of its own, Eric saw a big black wooden house dominating the crossroads. It was a slightly different style from the others, less pretty, more . . . Eric searched for the word. More serious.

'This is the centre of the island, Eric. Welcome.'

Eric sat in Tor's house, his hands round a pottery mug of black tea.

The two women were introduced as Maya and Jane. Younger than Tor, older than Merle. Both were quiet, but seemed friendly enough as they'd made the tea in Tor's large kitchen. The other man is called Henrik, again younger than Tor, though it's hard to be sure. Eric guessed they get a lot of weather living on an island like Blessed.

Maybe the rumours are true, he thought. Maybe these people are living for ever, maybe Tor is a hundred and twenty, the others spring chickens of ninety-eight.

'If there's any way we can help you with your article,

anything you require,' said Henrik, 'you only need ask. We are the Wards of Blessed, and . . .'

Tor coughed, so quietly it was hard to believe that it was a signal, but Henrik stopped and corrected himself.

'Tor is *the* Ward of Blessed. We,' he nodded at Maya and Jane, and pointed to himself, 'are the other wards of the island. So you only need to speak to one of us and it will be arranged.'

'Thank you,' Eric said. 'You are all very kind.'

He wondered where Merle had gone.

It's not even as if she is beautiful, not in the way people usually mean. She's more than pretty, that's what he can say, but it's not that that has caught him. It is simply her face, her eyes. The moment he saw them something clicked. He suddenly realised what it was. He recognised her face. As if seeing an old friend, long forgotten, and that triggered something else inside him. A thought that bothered him.

His head swam.

'I'm tired,' he said. 'Excuse me. I'm tired, but I think I could do with some air before bed. Could I . . .?'

'But of course,' Tor replied. 'Why don't you explore the lanes and we'll come and get you when your house is ready. Don't go far.'

Eric stands at the top of a small but steep hill known as the Outlook, looking to the west, watching the sun fail to set, thinking about Merle. The path he has taken is an odd one – it is well made, as well made as any he has seen so far,

13

but it stops at the top of the hill by a thicket of bushes, and goes no further. He has taken a few steps off the path on to a rocky outcrop, from where he can see over the treetops of the woods, to the west.

Tor's questions about his parents come back to him, and he realises that it's been many years since he thought about them. Almost as if they were dead. And though they're not dead, they may as well be. He hasn't seen them or spoken to them in years. Not really since he was old enough to leave home, and go out into the world by himself.

Tor. What is it about the man? His eye is a little unsettling, maybe, but Eric knows there's something else. The man has been nothing but helpful, so what is it that makes Eric feel wary of him?

He brings back to mind the thought that bothered him at Tor's house. He recognised Merle's face.

Recognised. But that's not possible, because he has never seen her before.

As if to check, he pulls out his device, and is about to tap on OneDegree again, when he notices another oddity; he has no reception.

Of course, he's heard of places that have no signal, but he's never been to one.

A quiver runs through him as he realises that the device that runs his whole life has just turned into an expensive little box of plastic, silicon and glass.

He thinks about OneDegree, how it finds other lives, across the ether, and wonders if that can be done without a machine.

He looks out at the horizon again.

He has never been here, yet he feels he has met Merle before, and then, there is that other feeling, that somehow disturbs him even more.

Why, he thinks, do I have the feeling that I have come home?

'I don't think you'll find that works.'

He jumps, and spins round to see Merle approaching from the path.

He puts it away, feeling stupid. He takes the chance to look at her as she approaches, wishing he had more than these few moments to work out what it is about her. He fails.

'I think you're right,' he says as she comes up to him. 'But how do you get by? Without devices?'

'We get by just fine,' says Merle, laughing. 'We simply do things differently here.'

'Like having no cars?'

'I believe we are not the only place that has no need for cars,' she says.

'I don't know about need,' Eric says, 'but yes, since petrol became so scarce, there are many places that use alternatives.'

He wonders why he can't find anything better to talk to her about than petrol. Cars. Devices. They are alone now, for the first time. He can almost feel her body heat, she's standing so close.

'You came here by our steam-boat, of course.'

Eric nods.

And before that, he thinks, I flew on a good old-fashioned plane, chewing thousands of gallons of aviation fuel. And a ticket with a price that proved it.

Still, if he gets this story, his expenses will be well worth it.

'This is a small island, and a small community. There is no need to rush. We walk. If matters are really pressing, one can usually borrow a bicycle.'

Eric tries to suppress a laugh. He doesn't mean to be rude, but the serious look on Merle's face amuses him.

She doesn't seem annoyed, or if she is, she doesn't show it.

'Look,' she says, pointing into the sky. Not down near the sun, but up, the moon is visible, a pale pink disc against the dark blue heavens. 'It's the flower moon.'

'The what?'

'It's the old name for this month's moon,' Merle explains. 'The flower moon. Do you see how pink it is?'

'That's quite a sight,' Eric agrees.

They say nothing for a while, just staring at the moon, ancient, as old as time, and unknowable. Mysterious. Powerful.

Merle whispers, some lines from an old song.

'*And none of you stand so tall, a pink moon gonna get you all.*'

She stirs herself.

'Your house is ready,' she says. 'It's late. I'm sure you're tired.'

Eric is *very* tired.

'Thank you,' he says. He means it. 'It's generous of you to offer a whole house for me to live in.'

He thinks about his expenses again.

'A room is all I need really,' he continues, 'and of course, I can pay you for your troubles.'

'That won't be necessary. The wards have offered you a house, by the meadow. It's comfortable, but you must let us know if there's anything else we can do.'

They walk through the lanes, and Eric keeps trying to remind himself it's night-time, which is hard because it's almost as bright as day.

'Doesn't it mess with your sleep?' he asks. 'The constant day?'

'You have no idea! But we have ways round it. Thick curtains, black-out blinds. That helps. And tea, that tea you had will help you sleep. Here.'

She stops, and points to Eric's new home.

It is small but stylish, a blue wooden house, with its own garden, neatly cut grass, heavily blooming rose bushes. Honeysuckle climbs the wall and over a window on the second floor. Other flowers whose names he does not know. The name of the house is painted at the gate. *The Claw*.

'Strange name,' Eric muses, half aloud.

'It's from the old dialect. It refers to a type of fishing boat, I believe.'

Suddenly Merle wrinkles her nose, and sneezes.

'Grass pollen,' she says, and sneezes again.

'Bless you.'

Merle looks at Eric.

'Don't say that.'

'Why not?'

'We don't say that here, on the island. We think it's . . . bad luck.'

'That's strange.'

'Just another one of our little differences,' Merle says.

She smiles, and turns to leave. Eric fights the urge to say something to Merle. Something meaningful. But he cannot think what.

'Good night, Eric Seven,' she calls as she goes. 'The house is unlocked.'

She stands for a moment more by the gate, and then is gone.

Eric imagines that he sees her lips move. He imagines that she says one word to him.

You.

He wonders what he would have felt if she really had said it.

Eric opens the door to his house, and finds his way to the bedroom. By the time he gets there, he is feeling lousy, his head swimming, from tiredness and being somewhere new, and the scent of those flowers, and he can taste the tea in his mouth.

He passes out on the bed, his thoughts tumbling down a deep, deep chasm that has opened beneath the place where his mind sits.

One final thought comes to him as he goes, and then is lost in the tumbling storm of his mind-stream.

He has been on Blessed for several hours.

He has met a few people, and seen many more.

But he has not seen a single child.

Four

E ric sleeps well.
   When he wakes, he feels much better. Wonderful in fact.

He opens his eyes and is surprised to find the room in total darkness. First he thinks that night has finally come, then remembers that there will be no such thing as night here for a month or two at least. Not properly.

He stumbles to the window, and pulls the curtains back.

It is still dark; his hands reach and touch the black-outs Merle spoke of, and finding a cord to one side, he pulls them up.

Bright, strong sunshine floods into the room, and he shuts his eyes and waits till they adjust.

When they do, he is overwhelmed by the beauty of the island.

His bedroom window looks to the south and to the east. Below him is another small slice of heaven. Pretty coloured houses, little lanes, tall birches swaying in a gentle wind, and everywhere flowers.

Flowers.

People are walking in the lanes, they call to each other, and pause to chat at the tiny toy-town intersections. From somewhere he cannot see he can hear music. And singing.

It sounds like a dozen voices, a haunting, conflicting yet beautiful melody, to a simple accompaniment of a guitar and accordion. He strains to catch the words, but they are blown away.

The sky overhead is blue, and everywhere there are flowers.

Eric feels wonderful. All grogginess from the night before has vanished. All thoughts of the night before are forgotten.

But he feels hungry, amazingly hungry. He wonders if they will have been thoughtful enough to have left some food for him, and he goes downstairs, where he finds not just food, but a whole breakfast laid out on the kitchen table. A pot of coffee is warming on the stove.

'Hello?' he calls, turning about him. 'Hello? Is anyone there?'

There is no one, so he sits down and eats as if he has never eaten before. He has bread, and honey, and cheeses, and there is some tasty dried meat, and apple juice, and then there's the coffee. And in the middle of the table is a vase of small pretty yellow flowers, freshly picked from the meadow.

Flowers.

Flowers, he thinks. Flowers.

He was supposed to do something about flowers.

But he cannot remember what it is.

He happily finishes his breakfast.

Five

———

Eric checks his watch, and is surprised to see it has gone noon.

He has slept for a long time. He walks out into the day and decides to go for a stroll. He passes people, tending their gardens, just walking, or doing nothing. They smile, and he nods back at them, a little shyly.

He finds himself climbing a lane through the trees that cluster to one side of his house, and then descending on the other side, the woodland gives way and there is the sea before him and another rocky stretch of coastline.

He is suddenly taken with a massive urge to swim. It's a hot day, and the sea looks inviting. He explores for a while and before long finds a tiny hidden cove among the rocks. He looks around. He has neither towel nor trunks with him, but the place is deserted. He's sure he can't be seen from the path he came down by.

He undresses quickly and eases into the water from a warm rock. It feels good, stinging cold at first, but the freshness of the cold salty water is delicious.

He comes out, and this time, finds a higher rock to dive from.

He plunges in, through the safe water near the surface to a colder, darker, more dangerous world beneath. Darkness beneath the beauty.

As he surfaces, water runs down his face, across his eyes, trickles from his ears, and as it washes the clouds from his mind, he remembers.

'What the hell am I doing?' he actually says aloud, and clambering up the rocks, makes towards his clothes.

He stops, staring at them. He knows he dropped them in a pile where he undressed. Now, they're laid out neatly, spread flat, to warm on the sunny rocks. He looks around, but can see no one. Nothing.

Shaking his head, he pulls his clothes on, though he is still dripping wet.

He tries to clear his head as he walks back to his house, remembering now why he came here, and that he's supposed to be working.

He ignores friendly greetings as he heads back to The Claw, and makes his way to his room, where he grabs his device and a notepad, a pen, sitting down at the bedside table. He thinks he hears a noise. The gate clicks, and he lifts his head waiting to hear approaching footsteps. None come, and then, determined not to be distracted, he concentrates again.

'What was I thinking?' he says again, staring out of the window. He starts to work.

He goes through what he knows.

Blessed Island, an obscure self-governed community in the farthest north. Population unknown, but small. Economic production? The island was once home to a fishing fleet, now vanished. However they make their money now, Eric has already seen that it isn't tourism. There's nowhere for anyone to stay for a start, and when they do have someone to stay, they don't charge.

So how do they make their money?

What do they do here? Without warning, his mind feels fuggy again, and his memory is struggling, though he knows there is something else he was sent to investigate.

He gets up and walks round the room, trying to clear his head.

It comes to him that he had some notes, that he had prepared before he came, and he thumbs the power on his device.

It boots, and he goes straight to Notes.

He reads.

Flowers.
Blessed Island is believed to be home to the only surviving population of a very rare orchid: the Blessed Dragon Orchid, Latin name Orchidae dracula beati. Also known as the Dracula Orchid.

Eric had smiled when he'd first read its creepy name, then realised that Dracula had nothing to do with vampires, but merely means Little Dragon. But Beati. He'd had to look that up, and found it was the Latin for Blessed.

Little Blessed Dragon.

He'd found pictures of it, and despite the apparently innocent meaning of its name, it did look a bit weird, scary even. More like an animal than a flower, a spiky dragon-headed thing, with purple petals and a blood-red throat at its heart.

The rumours hold that the islanders have recently, or otherwise, discovered that the orchid has health-giving properties, that it promotes well-being, and energy. That it regenerates damaged cell tissue. That it could even extend life.

That the islanders have extracted an elixir of life from the flower, and are selling it untrialled, and therefore illegally, for exorbitant sums, to the super-rich of the western world.

That is why he has come here.

He'd spoken to someone on a visit to London who claimed he knew someone who was using the drug, but that was just the problem. It was all someone, who knew someone, who knew someone. Hearsay.

Now he's at the source of the story, but he's already learned from OneDegree that this place might be less connected to the outside world than most.

He flicks through the notes on his device, looking for a map he knows he stored. He finds it, and just as it flashes onto the screen, the battery gives out.

He shakes his head. He goes to his bag, and rummages around for his charger, but can't find it.

Silly, he thinks.

He hunts through the bag again, in all its side pockets, and the little compartment at the front.

He still can't find it. He knows he packed it because he used it on the plane.

He takes everything from his bag, slowly, trying to keep calm, telling himself it will tumble out of a sock any moment.

But it doesn't.

24

He looks at everything he has brought with him, spread on the bed, and he comes to the conclusion that someone has taken his charger away in the night.

Something cold slices into his mind.

He is afraid.

Six

'How is your article coming along, Mr Seven?'

Tor smiles at him. Always the same smile, as if waiting patiently for something.

'Very good,' Eric lies quickly. 'I would like to borrow a bike, however.'

Does he imagine that Tor hesitates for a fraction of a second before answering?

'Of course,' Tor says. 'May I offer you some tea?'

Without waiting for an answer, Tor ducks into the kitchen in the Cross House.

Eric feels frustration rising. He has decided not to mention the missing charger, but he's not going to be side-tracked.

He hears voices in the kitchen, and is about to creep closer over the wooden floor, when Tor reappears, cup of tea in hand.

'Here you are,' he says.

Eric takes it, somewhat churlishly.

'I usually take milk.'

'This is better without it,' Tor says, smiling. 'Trust me. This is a special variety, with a touch of root in it too. Now . . .'

'I'm sorry, I don't mean to be rude, but I am here to

work and I really could do with a bicycle to get around. And a map of the island.'

Tor holds up his hand.

'I have arranged the bicycle. It will be here shortly. Why don't you sit while you wait, and drink your tea? And I'm sure I can find a map for you somewhere. You must be a little tired still, I think, no?'

As soon as Tor mentions it, Eric does feel a wave of exhaustion come over him.

'The tea will help,' Tor says, as Eric sits down on a very old but very comfortable sofa. 'Now, where's that map?'

Eric drinks his tea.

Seven

E ric is glad to escape from Tor's house.
   He still doesn't know why the man bothers him,
but he does. He cannot work out why, when he's been
nothing but kind, and helpful.

Eric straddles his bike at the intersection of Homeway
and Crossway, and studies the map.

He decides to start again, at the beginning, and to head
back north to the quay. From there he will cycle south,
methodically exploring every lane and path. If they are
producing some elixir here, they must be growing large
quantities of the Dracula Orchid, which means a field, or
maybe a series of glasshouses. He doesn't know much about
orchids, not even if they can be cultivated en masse, but he
knows they are rare and delicate things, that tolerate only
very finely balanced conditions in which to grow. In any
case, it's an incredibly rare variety that grows so far north.

He sets off, and suddenly he is smiling again.

Much of his life is spent travelling, investigating stories
all over the world. Most of the time he's on his own, and
sometimes the trips he has to make are hard, dangerous
even. With no one waiting for him at home, not even any
truly life-long friends, he often feels like a ghost, drifting
over the face of the earth, rootless. If he died, it would
be weeks before anyone even knew, let alone cared. Just

for once, his journey has taken him somewhere lovely, somewhere warm, and beautiful. He starts laughing.

He laughs at the fact that he's able to free-wheel the whole way to the quayside. He whizzes along, the bees humming around his head and around the flowers that burst with life on every side.

Birds call, and his bike picks up speed. He sticks his feet out sideways and feels the joy of the simple pleasure of free-wheeling in the sunshine. He plays a little game, seeing how long he dares shut his eyes for, and as he does, the image in his mind is, inexplicably, Merle's soft neck. And his lips brushing it.

He snaps out of it, reminding himself he is here to work, but nevertheless, as he arrives at the quay, there is still a smile on his face.

The smile gets bigger when he sees Merle approaching.

'How is your article coming?' she says brightly.

'Everyone is so concerned for me!' he says, laughing.

Merle seems puzzled.

'And why wouldn't we be?' she says. She tips her head on one side and Eric swears he can feel his heart swell.

'I'm sorry,' he says, 'it's just that the rest of the world is different from here. People aren't so thoughtful. So generous. It's all rush-rush, and no time for please and thank you. It's . . .'

'I understand,' Merle says. 'It's different.'

'Well, so it is,' he says. He stops, trying to think of something to say to keep the conversation going. He looks down. 'Tor lent me this bike.'

Inwardly he groans at another stunningly ineloquent conversation piece. But it doesn't matter. Ever so gently,

Merle puts her hand on his forearm.

'I found you,' she says. That's all.

Before she can say more, something distracts her and she looks over his shoulder.

'Forthwith the devil did appear,' she sighs, 'for name him and he's always near.'

'Pardon?' says Eric, but Merle does not reply. He turns to see Tor standing behind him.

'You got here quickly,' Eric says bluntly.

'I strolled up from the Cross House,' Tor replies. 'You forget, it is a small island. It doesn't take so very long to get anywhere. Even on foot, and even for an old man, as I am.'

Again, Eric wonders how old Tor is. How old anyone really is on Blessed.

'I have some business to discuss with Merle,' Tor says, smiling.

He waits. Fixing Eric with his one good eye.

'Oh, of course,' Eric stammers, and nods. 'Well, I must get on. See you later.'

His eyes are on Merle alone as he says this, hoping for some reaction from her.

For the briefest of moments there is a look of such trembling intensity on her face, and in that moment, he realises he was wrong. He looks at her lips and her eyes, the curve of her eyebrow, and realises that she *is* beautiful.

'Bye, Eric,' she says.

He nods, backs away, and cycles off.

I found you.

Was there some deeper meaning behind what she said?

He wants to believe there is.

Eight

Eric explores late into the afternoon.

He finds nothing, at least, nothing that he is looking for.

The orchids, or a production facility maybe, a homespun lab of some sort. He supposes he will know it when he sees it. That's how it is in his job, and he has always quietly thought to himself that that is why he has been successful in his work. That, and something less easy to admit, that maybe he is never satisfied. Neither in life, or work, nor in love – he always wants more. It has made him a good journalist, this desire in him to search for more, but although he knows it deep inside, he has never admitted to himself that this same thing has left him alone, with a heart that nervously beats for fear of never finding. But something just clicks when he's on the right track of a story, something just clicks. Like something clicked when he saw Merle's face.

He finds himself back at the Cross House, and pulls out the map again, trying to decide where to look next.

It is getting late, but that does not matter, because it will not get dark. The flower moon is rising above the hill. He studies the map that Tor gave him.

It looks hand drawn, but he can see it is printed, and there's a title and a price on the back of it. There is something about it that nags at him, but he's finding it so hard to think. He wonders if he's getting ill, it's twice now that his mind has felt like this. Cloudy.

With an effort, his head clears, and into his memory comes the image of the map of Blessed, the one that he'd saved on his device.

He realises that the map in front of him is not the same as the one he had recorded back at the office.

That one had two halves, a very distinct shape, like the two wings of a butterfly, though the western half slightly smaller, giving it a lopsided look. The two halves were joined by a narrow strip of land.

Eric looks at the paper map in his hand. Only the eastern half of the island is printed. Half the island is missing.

Now why, he thinks, would they print a map of only half the island?

That would be stupid. Unless, unless, unless you wanted to keep half of it secret.

He knows he's on to something.

And he knows his journalist's mind is working well, when he immediately makes another connection.

That path, up the hill, last night.

It was a path that went nowhere, or at least, seemed to.

The path was somewhere off Crossway. He turns his bike, and begins to pedal.

Nine

H e is half way up the short but ridiculously steep hill when he stops, for two reasons. First, the slope is just too steep to cycle up, even standing on the pedals in lowest gear. His thighs scream at him to stop, but there's something else. This exertion on the bike makes him think about the cycling he has done so far that day.

He remembers free-wheeling all the way to the quay. And then he remembers coming back again, but he can't remember cycling very hard to do so. In fact, he's pretty sure he free-wheeled much of the way back. If not all the way. He thinks about all the other places he's been to and now that he comes to think of it, he cannot remember actually having to push the pedals at all, anywhere, not until he came to this ludicrous hill. It doesn't make sense, and for a second he wonders if this is all some extended dream.

The only other possibility is that the bike is possessed.

He looks down at it, then shakes his head.

'Well, well,' he says, giving up trying to understand. 'So it is.'

Bending his head low he pushes the bike to the top of the hill, near to the point where he'd scrambled up to the outcrop the night before. He leans the bike by the rock, and starts to explore. The path, such as it is, seems to stop right by the bush.

It is a dense thicket, shrubs and trees, and low ground coverage. He tries to lift a branch and force his way in, but it is hard going.

The branches push back at him with thorny spines, and he thinks that even a barbed-wire fence would be easier to deal with. A branch whips him in the face and he's angry. Putting his head down, heedless of the pain, he shoves through the bushes.

He lands on his hands and knees, in a tiny clearer space.

There is a face looking at him, right in front of his nose. Only it's not a face. He's looking at a rock, upon which is painted two blue dots, each surrounded by a white circle, like eyes. Now he looks closely, he sees that the dots are painted on either side of a protrusion of the rock, making it look like a primitive creature of stone, a lizard or a dragon, with an eye facing each way.

His gaze drifts into the woodland, and he almost jumps when, a little way off, he sees another of the rock faces, with just one eye this time, looking sideways.

He hears voices, and freezes.

Looking back through the undergrowth, he can make out figures standing by the bike. Two or three people. He cannot make out what they're saying; they speak quietly, but then he sees their legs moving from the path to his lookout point, up on the outcrop.

He decides that he doesn't want to get caught here, and taking his chance, pushes his way quickly back, which, it turns out, is easier than forcing his way in.

34

Glancing to his left, he grabs the bike, and he's free-wheeling fast before they have a chance to return to the path.

At the bottom of the hill, he turns right and finds himself outside the Cross House.

He looks at his watch, and it's late, but he decides he's too tired to care about offending Tor.

He leans his bike at the gate, and walks up the path. It's another hot evening and the windows are open. He's about to knock on the door when he hears voices coming from inside. Raised voices.

He hesitates, then slips round the side of the house, on a veranda that runs round the corner.

He stands by the kitchen window, trying not to look as if he's spying, in case anyone sees him.

He hears Tor's voice, and another that he thinks is Henrik. There are female voices too. Maya and Jane presumably. And is that Merle?

Yes, he's sure of it.

'We will do everything as we always do.'

That's Tor. The man he thinks is Henrik speaks next.

'But will it do any good? We have tried for so long!'

'We will do everything as we always do,' Tor repeats. He sounds angry. 'We will do as our ancestors did.'

There is a confusion of voices then, everyone talking at once.

Then Merle says, 'I agree with Henrik. We ought to try something different.'

A pause. Then Tor again, more softly.

'Merle, my child. You are speaking of things you do not

35

understand. You are our treasure. You are the youngest of us, and for that alone, we treasure you and respect you. But you do not know all there is to know.'

The youngest of us?

Eric remembers that he's seen no children on the island. Not one. And Merle, a young woman, certainly is the youngest person he has seen since his arrival.

'You do not know everything!' Tor repeats.

'And do you?'

He can hear Merle's sudden defiance, and he can feel the terrible rage that springs into Tor right there and then.

'Enough! I have spoken. I am the Ward of Blessed Island, and I have spoken. You all have your duties. See that you do them, and do them well. Now go!'

Again a babble of voices, and then Tor must have beaten the table or the floor, for there is a loud bang, and silence is restored.

Tor's voice comes again, but so deep and so low that Eric cannot decipher his words.

He's had enough, and walking quickly round to the front of the house, he knocks, and without waiting to be invited, opens the door and walks in.

He almost bumps into Merle, who is in the hallway.

She opens her mouth in surprise, but before she can speak, Tor appears in the doorway.

'Do you usually enter people's houses without being invited, Mr Seven?'

His voice is steady and firm, there is none of the anger Eric has just heard.

'I . . . No, I . . .' he stops, tries again. 'I heard raised voices. I came to see that everything is all right.'

Tor pauses.

'That is thoughtful of you, but we are quite well.'

'You have been so kind to me,' Eric says, smoothly. 'It was the least I could do.'

'But I think you are mistaken,' Tor says. 'Quite well. You are well, Merle, are you not?'

Merle nods. Without a trace of worry or fear she smiles at Tor.

'Yes, very well, Ward. Very well.'

'So there. You see. There is nothing to concern yourself over. Merle, you had better get on home.'

Without another word, without looking at either of them, Merle leaves, slipping through the front door and closing it behind her. Eric watches her disappear through the doorway, noticing her height. She is tall, he hadn't noticed that before.

'Now, Eric. How is your article coming along? You've had a long day.'

Eric is caught, not knowing what to do. Having stormed to Merle's rescue, he now finds himself being offered another cup of tea by the enemy.

He follows Tor into the living room, and vaguely notices that the others have melted away into the evening. He sees the comfortable old sofa, and suddenly feels very tired again.

'Tea?' asks Tor.

Eric looks at Tor.

'Yes, please.'

'Milk?'

'Oh, no, thanks,' says Eric. 'You were right, it's much better without.'

Tor nods, and backs off into the kitchen.

'I'm so glad you agree,' he says.

When he comes back, he watches quietly as Eric drinks the tea. Tiredness washes over him, but somehow the bitter taste of the tea makes it a pleasurable feeling.

All he has to do, all he has to do now, he thinks, is make the short journey home, and then he can sleep.

Ten

Eric sleeps late.

It's the curtains, the blinds, he tells himself.

'Nothing to wake me up,' he says.

He decides to set an alarm for the next morning, not remembering his device is dead, nor that his charger is missing.

He showers, for a long time, then goes downstairs to eat another huge and delicious breakfast. At the back of his mind is a vague thought, a mere feeling, like an itch that wants to be scratched. But it's so faint and he's soon able to ignore it. There are firm fresh raspberries in a bowl on the table. He takes a mouthful, then a few mouthfuls more, until the whole bowl is finished.

He sits back, and sighs happily.

Only then does he see a short handwritten note leaning against a vase of flowers in the centre of the table.

It's a lovely day for a swim. The south pier is the best.

He picks the note up, slowly.

'So it is!' he says.

After breakfast he rolls up a towel from the bathroom and sets off, to the south.

As far as he can remember, he hasn't been to the far south of the island yet, and it doesn't even occur to him why he can't remember if he has or not. Nor does he realise that he has lost track of time, though he only arrived a few days ago.

Homeway twists and turns past more colourful houses, until he reaches a junction, where a tiny wooden sign points the way to the pier. He follows this smaller path for a few minutes more, and then he sees the sea in front of him.

It's beautiful. It's so beautiful, it takes his breath away. It's not spectacular, it's not jaw dropping, it's simply a lovely sight, that makes the heart glad that such places exist. The greys and browns of the rocks, the trees and the wild grass, the sea, waiting for him, and only for him; the place is utterly deserted, he can see neither people nor houses.

He goes down to the pier and, taking his shoes off, sits with his feet in the water for a while, then undresses and slides into the water, swimming far out away from the jetty.

He turns and looks at the island, and feels that little itch at the back of his head again. He swims closer to the pier, ducking underwater for long spells.

Suddenly, as he surfaces, someone is there in the water with him, an arm's length away.

All he sees at first is a splash as they dive in, but moments later, a head and shoulders break the surface in a tumble of water.

It's Merle. Her wet hair is drawn back, and down her neck.

Neither of them say anything, and as Eric treads water, Merle edges closer.

There's that gently intense look on her face again, that's something he does remember, something that is pushing through the clouds in his mind.

She reaches out a hand, treading water, and their fingertips meet.

She whispers, just loud enough to be heard over the shushing of the waves.

'I followed you.'

Eric hesitates for a moment, wondering, but then he's laughing, and Merle is too.

'You.'

They swim together, far out to sea.

They duck under the surface, twisting and turning, hand in hand where they can, and gliding through the deep, Eric's lips brush her neck, just once. Finally they come up for air. And when they do, they do so laughing.

'This is ridiculous!' shouts Eric, and Merle shrugs, and smiles, as if to say, so what?

Eric tries again.

'Have we done this before?' he calls.

Merle is a few strokes away. He pulls his way over to her, and tries again.

'Have we done this before?'

Merle shrugs again.

'I feel like we've done this before,' he says, intently. 'But a long time ago. A very long time ago.'

She's gone, under the water again.

Eric thinks about his life, something he usually avoids, because it has not always been an easy one. He wonders if a few moments of utter and total joy can be worth a lifetime of struggle.

Maybe, he thinks. Maybe, if they're the right moments.

They swim some more, and finally, exhausted, climb onto the rocks to dry in the warm sun.

Eric turns and holds Merle's hands. He looks at his hands, a little older than hers. He looks at her younger ones. What if it were the other way round? What if his were the younger hands? Would it matter?

He asks himself why *this* hand, is *his* hand. Could it have been someone else's? And why is that *her* hand? Does it matter? And what if she were different? No, he thinks, as these strange and somehow foolish questions roll around in his head. No, it wouldn't matter. Even if she were different, she would still be *she*.

'This is ridiculous,' he says again, and she sits up, and gently takes his head between her hands.

'Why?' she says. 'Why is it? Why is it any more ridiculous than a thousand things? That the earth spins round the sun, that water can eat a mountain away, that a salmon can swim a thousand miles across the ocean to find the very stream it was born in. It's not ridiculous. It's just . . . how it is.'

Suddenly she fumbles in her clothes, spread on the rocks, and finds a watch.

'I have to go.'

'But, stay . . .'

'I'm sorry,' she says, shaking her head.

She will not be persuaded otherwise, and Eric watches her clothe her naked skin and then, like a dream that drifts out of reach on waking, she is gone.

He dozes on the rocks, the sense of Merle around and inside him, seeing her slender limbs, smelling the salt in her hair, imagining that the warmth of the sunshine is her hands on his skin. He realises that for the first time in a very long time, his heart is beating slow and calmly. Peacefully.

He wakes some time later, with that itch once more.

Something starts to rise to the top of his mind.

He walks home, trying to get a hold of it, whatever it is. He's sure that it's something he's supposed to be doing.

As he enters the house, he thinks he hears the back door, the kitchen door, shut.

He shrugs.

Maybe just the door slamming in the wind, though he doesn't get as far as noticing that there is no wind.

He hangs his towel over the balustrade to dry in the sun, and comes back into the kitchen, where he sees that someone has left him a jar of that tea, and he decides the best thing to do is have a drink, to think about whatever it is he's supposed to be thinking about.

He brews the tea, not really noticing that it has a slightly different taste, that it has become a little stronger.

And so he drinks, and the forgetting begins again.

Eleven

The days pass.

The island is so beautiful, Eric thinks, every day as he wakes up, and every night as he goes to sleep. He's had Tor bring him some more of that tea in a tall glass jar, and he's quite proud of the little ritual he has created for himself every evening.

The days pass.

The sun burns strongly, the summer is young and fresh, the leaves and the grass bright, and vivid.

Eric passes his time walking round the island. He nods at people he's getting to know, and smiles. From time to time he stoops and sniffs at a flower in this garden or that.

Merle comes to see him sometimes, and he is just as happy to see anyone else as her. There was something about her, that's all. That's how the thought forms in his head. There was something about her. But it doesn't matter. Not really. She seems a little distracted, frustrated at times, and Eric starts to wonder what the cause might be, but he decides that that doesn't matter either. She ought to be like everyone else on the island. Sometimes she seems to look at him almost accusingly, but he can't fathom why, or what he might have done. He hasn't got the energy, his mind is too slow, and he soon gives up worrying about it.

The people are smiling and beautiful, and Eric feels happy and beautiful too.

His only other visitor during that time is not a person.

One morning he finds a rabbit sitting in the middle of the path to his door. He looks closely and realises it's not a rabbit but a hare, long and lean. It's sitting side on to him, but is clearly watching him. Waiting.

He moves forward, expecting it to startle and bolt, but it does not. Puzzled, he makes a jump at it. It still stays exactly where it is. He is about to go right up to it, but something about its stare is unnerving, and in the end it is Eric who gives way to the hare, circling around it to go for a walk.

When he comes home that afternoon, the hare has gone.

The days pass.

One day melts into the next, the endless sun smoothing the journey round the calendar into one long chorus of joy. Of beauty, of joy, and of forgetting. Always forgetting.

The days pass.

Twelve

I t is the middle of what should be the night, when Eric suddenly wakes up, dreaming he is drowning.

He throws himself upright and out of bed, and cannot understand why there is actually liquid in his mouth. He falls onto the floor, choking, spluttering, retching some water that he has sucked into his windpipe.

The bedroom door is ajar. Does he hear, or does he imagine footsteps on the wooden staircase? He stumbles downstairs and finds the front door wide open, but there is no one there. He scans up and down the lane, and across the meadows. But there is no one there.

Warily, and still spluttering, he shuts the door, and makes his way back to bed.

His blinds are drawn, and as he switches on the light in the bedroom, he sees a piece of paper on the floor, right in the middle of the rug by his bed.

It is a little damp from his choking, but the words on the paper are clear enough.

Wake up and remember. You were right. The answer lies beyond the hill.

He looks at it blankly, and shakes his head.

'Well, so it is,' he says.

He stares at the note for a long time, trying to think

what to do, trying to think. He's so tired, though, so tired, and another wave of lethargy sweeps into him.

He gets back into bed, deciding the only thing is to forget all about it, and switching off the light, he shuts his eyes.

About five seconds later, the liquid that has made its way into his stomach gets to work, and then he's out of bed again.

He doesn't have time to get to the bathroom before he is violently and repeatedly sick on the floor.

His body heaves and shudders, aches and wails, and when it is over, he crawls back into bed, where he spends a grim night, half awake, half dreaming.

Is it this living nightmare, or is it whatever he was forced to drink in his sleep, that triggers a flood of memories, memories from long ago, of other nightmares?

Nightmares that terrified not just him, but his devout and strict parents too. Blood-soaked dreams that came night after night as a teenager, dreams that upon waking seem more real than the drab surroundings of his mundane room, his grey house, his ever more distant mother and father. His life.

Blood-soaked nightmares. Of another time. Of another place. Another life.

Thirteen

———

It is the middle of the day when Eric finally feels he has enough energy to stagger from his bed, but when he does, something has cleared in his head. He has a long hot shower, trying to think, think more clearly.

Automatically, his hand reaches for the shower controls. He turns the power up, and reaches for the temperature control, and slowly, fighting the urge not to, he takes the temperature down, and down and down, until he is showering in what feels like ice water. It's agony, but he forces himself on, until his whole body is shaking with the cold, then heaving in great spasmodic shudders. He looks at his hands. They are virtually blue.

He falls backwards out of the shower, and shaking on the bathroom floor, everything comes back to him.

Images swim through his head – they are the broken pieces of fractured memories; the journey to Blessed, the flowers, his device. Merle.

He lies for an age on the floor, holding a picture of her face in his mind. Merle.

The answer lies beyond the hill.

He looks out of the window. It's very quiet, he guesses it's a Sunday, though he's not sure any more.

This is the perfect time. In five minutes he is whizzing

fast on his bike, fully aware that he is having to pedal hard, as he makes his way up the steep, steep hill that he knows leads to the western half of the island.

As he cycles, he repeats her name in his head, using it as a mantra to keep his mind clear. Merle, Merle, Merle.

At the top, he takes time to look behind him, checking to see if he has been followed, and satisfied that he has not been, forces his way back through the undergrowth, looking for the eyes on the rocks.

He finds the first quickly, and crawls on hands and knees to the second and then the third.

By the time he gets to the fourth pair of eyes, he is able to stand, and at the sixth, he is in open country again.

The land slopes down in front of him, a mixed terrain of grasses, rocky patches, clumps of purple heather, and marsh. He follows the eyes, and very soon, he turns a corner, cresting a large outcrop, and there lies the narrow causeway that will take him to the western half of Blessed.

Again he glances behind, and seeing no one, hurries on, half running, half stumbling over the uneven ground.

The causeway could be man-made. He's not sure. It looks natural enough now, but it's not much more than a jumble of large boulders and smaller rocks, against which a small beach of sand has formed. It seems that there are really two islands here, the one severed from the other in some geological moment millions of years ago.

The distance between them is short, and in a dozen strides he's across and into a very different landscape.

There are no trees here.

He follows the eyes on the rocks, a series leading him on, painted who knows how many years ago, and within moments he discovers the first secret of the western half of Blessed. The flowers.

He sees just one at first, then a couple. He stumbles on and sees a dozen more, and then, turning a corner in the rocks, hundreds. Thousands.

He knows it must be the Little Blessed Dragon Orchid. It is as mysterious as its name. A tall stem, with odd, curly star-shaped leaves clinging to it, and the flower itself, a dark purple-black thing, weirdly contorted. He looks closely, and can indeed imagine that it is a dragon's head; there are even little bumps on the upper petal that look like horns, and a long black tongue protrudes from the mouth of the upper and lower petals, like that of a dragon, black with poison and evil.

He goes to pick one, but something stays his hand. Even the scent of the flowers makes his senses swim, and he stands up, deciding to move on.

The ground dips and rises again, and the eyes pick up once more. It seems obvious to follow them, and after a short scramble along the rocks, he sees something that takes his breath away.

There is a church in front of him.

It's like no church he's ever seen, but he knows it can't be anything else.

It is wooden, of a single, high storey, with a pitched roof, which he is looking at side on. He is open-mouthed as he makes his way around the building, where a small tower or portico frames the entrance.

The place is a ruin, he can see that, and has obviously not been used in years.

Like a traveller from another time, he staggers towards the waiting, gaping mouth of the building, and enters.

It feels like walking into the jaws of a huge wooden whale, and, if it is, he is swallowed whole by the beast.

The building itself is just a prelude.

What he sees next is the real surprise.

Where the altar should be, there is something massive, hidden.

A large cloth is draping something, hiding a long rectangular shape, which stands upright in the vast space of this temple.

He walks forward, feeling this is more unreal than any dream he has ever had. As he puts his hands out to the corner of the old, grey, tattered cloth, and pulls it away from whatever is underneath, it is as if he is hovering above himself, looking down, watching himself act.

What is underneath the cloth is a painting.

It is absolutely huge.

Dazed, Eric steps backwards again, trying to take it all in.

What he sees is a painting of such realistic horror, and yet at the same time such dreamlike variety, that his mind cannot comprehend it all at once.

There is a click on stone somewhere behind him, and he turns.

Tor stands in the doorway. Behind him Eric can see the other Wards.

Tor approaches, and immediately, Eric knows the game has changed.

51

'It is appropriate,' Tor says, 'that you should have seen it. You should know why the gods brought you here, to help us.'

He turns to his followers, and calls out instructions.

'Cover that up. And take him. The door, please!'

Suddenly the interior of the church fills with people, through unseen doors on either side of Eric.

While hands wrestle with the job of hiding the painting under the cloth once more, other hands close around Eric's wrists.

He tries to struggle, but there is no point. There are too many of them, even if he could wrestle free from their grasp for a moment, more hands would seize him.

The most frightening thing is their silence.

Their eyes do not even meet his, they just hold him firmly, three or four on either side.

'The door!' Tor cries again, and now real fear stabs Eric.

He has been taken beyond the painting-altar, and beyond, in the far wall of the church, another door is swung open.

Framed through the doorway, he can see the short distance to the sea, which burns brightly blue, but his eye is caught by what lies midway between the door and the sea.

It is a stone table.

Now he begins to struggle, quietly at first, then desperately.

Sheer fear surges from his stomach, into his mouth, making him want to be sick. He fights harder, but the more he struggles, the tighter the silent hands hold him.

He is steps from the stone table, and there is Tor at his

side, as he is pulled backwards towards it, kicking and now screaming, screaming.

They rip his shirt from his back, cast him onto the table, still pinning him fiercely. The stone rips into his skin, the sun almost blinds him, but his wide terror-staring eyes have time to see Tor draw a massive curved knife from somewhere.

He hands it to Henrik, who steps forward.

In another corner of his tunnelling vision, he sees a face he knows. A face he has known for always.

Merle looks down at him, tilting her head.

She whispers to him.

I followed you.

Eric screams, and though his mind has largely stopped working already, a final thought bleeds into it, following on from so very many strange thoughts.

I, thinks Eric Seven, have lived this before.

PART TWO

The Archaeologist

———

July 2011 – The Hay Moon

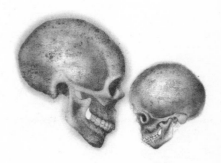

One

___

The boy looks at the archaeologist.

The archaeologist looks at the boy sometimes, too. But he has work to do, and limited money and limited time on the island.

It is hard to get funding for this kind of dig, small and obscure, and the travel expenses alone have eaten a big chunk out of his budget. It has cost him a fortune to get his team up here, though he has to admit he is actually embarrassed by how little they're charging him at the Wardhouse – the island's only guest house.

His team consists of three young graduates; again because they are cheap. Happily he can also say, hand on heart, that they are all three promising diggers. There's Nancy, an American he's known since she was an undergraduate; Isabella, a German girl, from Leipzig, and finally there's Mat, he's not from the island itself, but from the mainland, about a hundred miles south along the coast. In this remote part of the country, where distances are vast, that almost makes him a local.

But there's something about the boy that keeps taking Edward's attention away.

Every day, the boy comes to the dig, and stands on a low bump, one of many in this corner of the meadow, to get a good view of their work. Every day, around noon, a woman's voice calls to him from behind a nearby garden hedge, and he disappears, presumably for lunch. Half an hour later he reappears, takes up his spot on the mound, and spends the rest of the day watching.

He must be about sixteen Edward supposes, but he's big and strong, like a man twice that age. Edward suspects there is something wrong with him. He never speaks, though his lips are slightly parted much of the time, as if he is about to.

In his hands, like a small child, he is always, always, holding a soft toy. It is a brown hare. He holds it by its long ears, so that it droops from his big palm, dangling as if crucified.

Two

————

I t's nearly lunchtime, and though they have been here
a week, it's not going well. Again, because of money,
Edward has not been able to bring all the equipment he
would have liked.

On the first morning, Mat made a geophysical study of the
meadow, but the machine is lightweight, and gives rather
weak signals. While Mat walked up and down, through the
hay, sticking the sensors of the magnetometer in at regular
intervals, Edward, Nancy and Isabella crowded round
the laptop, trying to shield the screen from the sun's glare,
watching the scan of the field slowly emerge.

There wasn't much to go on, in truth, but Edward
decided to put two trenches in, a few metres apart, cutting
across some of the features produced by Mat's survey.

Edward watches them now, Nancy and Isabella,
working side by side in trench one. Nancy is tall and thin,
and kind of laid back. It's not that he thinks she is lazy, she
works as hard as the other two, it's just that everything she
does is done smoothly, easily. She is languid.

Isabella is a Goth. She has a pierced nose, and pink hair,
and always dresses in black. Odd earrings and strange
haircuts are not unusual among his profession, he knows,
but something about the way she has even managed to

develop a Goth field dress sense amuses him. But she's a good worker, always smiling. He once asked her if she wasn't too happy to be a Goth, really, and Isabella's excellent English let her down for once.

'Excuse me, please?' she'd said.

'Ignore me,' Edward had replied.

Mat, Edward has decided, is great. He is exactly what he seems to be. A tall, handsome, smiley boy from the countryside. One who's bright enough to have gone to the big city to get himself educated, but still come away without losing the trusting generosity of his people.

He talks carefully, as if considering everything, and is currently sporting a long beard and long hair, as if he's escaped from a seventies commune, though fortunately, one where they don't believe soap is the capitalists' tool of oppression.

Edward looks wistfully at Mat, and while the girls are pretty, Nancy particularly, it is Mat who he thinks about the most, because he wishes he'd been more like Mat when he was young.

If he'd been more like Mat, more confident, maybe he wouldn't have missed his chances in life, chances that sometimes only come along once. Sometimes there are single moments, he thinks, where your path divides, your life can go one way, so very different from another. Work out well, rather than be a failure. And if you miss those chances, he thinks, well, is that it?

His daydreams are disturbed by the woman's voice, calling from behind the hedge. He's never seen her; her garden backs onto the meadow, and he guesses the roof they can see beyond belongs to the boy's house.

She calls again.

'Eric!'

The boy leaves his mound, and goes in for lunch.

'Eric!'

Three

────────

That evening, the four archaeologists sit round the communal supper table at the Wardhouse.

Their landlord is a kindly old man, his wife is the cook; every evening they prepare and serve something simple, but delicious, all from the island, an island which seems to have everything its small population needs; sheep and goats for meat and milk, plenty of fish in the sea, lobsters, and even oysters. The fields are full of wheat, gently ripening, and there are orchards of fruit and fields of vegetables.

When Edward tried to offer a little more for their food and lodging the landlord would hear nothing of it.

'We do things differently here,' he'd said. 'What need have I of money? We have enough to cover our costs, and you are welcome visitors to our island. That is enough for us. We are always glad of visitors. Our little population has been dropping, you see. We used to be so many more, but not many babies are born on Blessed now.'

He'd smiled.

It's an extraordinary place, Edward has decided, and he wonders if it's the sort of place he'd like to retire to one day.

Maybe not. It might be a bit too simple, too quiet, even for his taste.

There's always something a little odd about remote places, he thinks. That sense that things happen differently. That's all it is, though earlier that day, a man began to cut the hay in the meadow, not with a tractor and swather, but with a scythe, as if this were 1911, not 2011.

And then there's the sun being up when it should be in bed. That would really mess with his sleep, and presumably it means in the winter it's perpetually dark, in return. That, he knows, he would *not* like.

They've been given permission to dig in the far end of the meadow, but only for two weeks; they have used half their time.

'Council of war,' Edward says, as they push away their plates. 'We need to find something, and quickly, or this dig will be written off and me with it.'

He smiles grimly.

'So, what do we do?'

Edward sighs. He's getting too old for long days in trenches with nothing to show for it. Once, he would have been excited anyway, just to have the trowel in his hands and the dirt under his fingernails. He looks at his three young keen accomplices.

'What do you guys think? Nancy, Isabella, how's life in trench one? Anything giving you cause for hope?'

Nancy shakes her head. Languidly.

'Nope. I know we found some resistance when Mat did the geophysics, but I'm dubious. No offence, Mat.'

Mat raises a hand.

'None taken. The equipment is . . .'

He stops, realising it's an implied criticism of Edward.

'. . . is rubbish,' Edward finishes. 'Don't worry, I apologise. It's all we could afford to transport.'

'I know this is not how you're supposed to do it,' Isabella says, 'but I'd love to have a go at some of the mounds round the edge of the field.'

Edward smiles inwardly at her excellent English idiom. *Have a go.*

'No, Isabella, that is not how we're supposed to do it. Proper archaeologists do not just *have a go* . . .'

Edward takes another drink of beer.

'Listen, I'm the boss. I'll have a think overnight and decide on a new plan for tomorrow, okay. At least we've had great weather. We can all go home with no artefacts, but lovely suntans. Even you, Isabella.'

They laugh.

Isabella pretends to glare at Edward, then smiles too.

'Yes, but you know, even if it was raining, I would like to bet that boy would still be standing there, watching us.'

They all agree.

'I think he's a bit creepy,' Nancy says.

'No. Don't be mean,' Mat says. 'He's okay. He's just interested.'

'But that toy. He must be fifteen, sixteen? That's a bit weird, isn't it?'

Edward nods, but says nothing.

'Yes,' says Isabella, 'but there is something about him. His eyes.'

'His eyes?' asks Nancy.

'Yes, his eyes,' Isabella says. 'His eyes . . . it seems like he knows everything, but is saying nothing.'

It is a remark that Edward finds disconcerting, because he had been about to say the very same thing.

Four

———

Next morning, Edward rises early, and helps himself to breakfast. He leaves a note for the others to join him at the site, and makes his way from the Wardhouse along the lane that runs beside the meadow, to the far end, where they have been digging.

He wants to stand at the site.

He has spent all night half-awake, wrestling with what decision to make. To abandon their two trenches, and to start new ones, or to persevere. It's a hard call, because there's no good reason to take one over the other.

And he has come early to the site, without the others, because he is too ashamed to confess that all he wants to do is stand there, and pray to the gods of Archaeology for a sign of what to do.

It's a slightly damp morning, but the sun is already up, of course, and the dew is starting to steam off the meadow. It will be another hot day.

Edward surveys the dig, and the meadow in general. He marvels at it, because if he had been God (though he's very glad he's not) and he were designing an island, Blessed is just what he would have drawn. It has two large natural harbours, one at each end of the island, and many other smaller ones round its shoreline. It has a high ridge of hills to the west, a lower one to the east, between them is a valley, which flattens out into the meadow where they are digging; a natural safe haven, and one that the Vikings used in the wintertime. A dig in 1902 found evidence of what is written in the old sagas, that after a long season of raiding to the south and west, they would hurry back to the island, and draw their longboats up onto the meadow, to overwinter in safety. He pictures the scene, imagines the men and women and the horses straining to drag their proud ships out of the water and into the meadow. Knarrs were big boats, but light enough to be carried short distances if need be. Nonetheless, it must have been quite a sight.

His attention snaps back to the present, and he thinks how far the world has come in a thousand years, how the island has changed in that time. And what will it be like in another thousand years? People, most people, always assume that civilisation steadily increases, that the world improves, becomes more peaceful, and it very often does. But if there's one thing he's learned in his days as an archaeologist, it's that this is not always the case. Sometimes, when civilisation falters, sometimes, things become more primitive again. More primitive, and more violent.

He stands with his hands on his hips, looking around at what they have done so far, and shakes his head.

'You should dig here,' says a voice behind him.

He turns to see the boy, Eric, in his usual spot. Edward suddenly wonders if he's been there all along, watching. He's so preoccupied that it's possible. He imagines the boy standing out all night, on the mound, bathing in silver moonlight.

Eric's pointing at his feet, his hare in his hand, as always.

'Sorry. Sorry, what did you say?'

But Eric does not answer, and though Edward tries gently to coax more out of him, he won't be drawn.

'Here?' says Edward, quietly. 'Here?'

He hears the others approaching, come out early to find him, and he backs away from Eric, as if he's feeling guilty about talking to him.

As the others arrive, he notices Eric move from the mound he always stands on, to another nearby.

'Well, boss?' says Nancy.

Edward pauses, wonders if he's about to say what he thinks he's about to say.

'Well. This is the decision. Mat and I are going to continue in trench two. But I would like, in fact, I would *love*, for you and Isabella to have a go at that mound. That one. Right there.'

There is a moment's silence in which no one says anything.

'There is good methodology for this?' Isabella asks. There's a twinkle in her eye.

Mat and Nancy both look at the grass.

Edward hesitates again, then smiles quickly.

'Absolutely! But we don't have time to discuss it. So let's dig people, yes? Dig!'

Five

There are moments in everyone's life, Edward thinks, when you just have to go with gut instinct. Especially at those times when you are faced with a fifty-fifty call, if there's even the slightest feeling tugging you one way, you'd better do what that feeling tells you.

That's what Edward convinces himself, and keeps repeating.

Time and again, Mat has to draw his attention back to the pit they're in, because Edward keeps stopping and looking across to where the girls are working, desperate to see something come up in the mound. Anything.

The morning wears on.

The mood worsens.

The only word they hear is spoken by the voice behind the hedge.

'Eric!'

Edward sighs.

'Let's take lunch too. We had an earlier start than normal.'

No one speaks.

Eric is back on his new mound sooner after lunch today. They're still chewing sandwiches and munching crisps when he reappears. It doesn't seem to bother him that they're not working, he stands watching, as interested as ever.

Finally Edward can stand it no longer.

'Come on,' he says. 'Let's give the boy something to be proud of.'

Nancy winks at Isabella and taps the side of her head, twice. Languidly.

In half an hour, Isabella shrieks.

She actually shrieks.

'Oh God! I think I found something.'

She has.

The afternoon goes by quickly, as the two girls begin to uncover their remarkable find. Edward and Mat cannot fit in the trench to help too, but they have abandoned their own dig; it is too exciting not to watch.

They have found a pile of stones, the sort of thing which does not seem very exciting to anyone but an archaeologist.

A pile of stones, but a particular sort of pile, a cairn, and Edward knows that it is very likely that there is a find underneath the cairn.

He has seen one before, and is impatient. But these

things have to be done properly. First the last of the soil must be removed from around the stones, and then the stones must be photographed, and drawn on grid paper, and only then will they be able to lift them, and find out for sure if what they have found is what Edward thinks it is; a Viking burial.

He has a doubt. He has a doubt because the cairn is small, much smaller than the burial sites he has seen before. He worked on one once that was vast. Beneath the stones lay the remains of a Viking longboat, most of the wood long rotted away, but obvious to the expert eye, nevertheless.

This one is small, and will barely have room for a single body, but something convinces Edward that he is right.

He paces up and down behind the girls, trying to stop himself from telling them what to do every five minutes. They know what to do, because he taught them himself. Mat is being more sensible, sitting on the grass by the girls' trench, helping them when he can, and sifting through the spoil when he can't.

Eric watches, wordlessly, though sometimes he lifts the hare to his lips.

Finally, they begin to raise the stones.

Edward holds his breath, and as they lever away enough of the stones, he turns and actually punches the air, silently.

'Yes,' he mutters under his breath.

Under the cairn is a cist; exactly what he had been hoping for, a box in the ground, with slabs of stone for walls. Essentially a primitive coffin.

A stone box, with a stone lid.

Edward steps into the trench.

71

'Okay now, people, this is going to take all of us.'

They cramp into the trench, at each side of the lid.

Their fingers curl under what lips of the lid they can feel. Their flesh touches stone that has not seen light for eleven centuries.

They are silent, but they catch each other's eyes, and see the suppressed excitement in each other.

Edward is wrong, however, even with all four of them, they cannot lift the lid.

Edward straightens his back, curses.

Then a shadow is cast over the trench, and he looks up to see Eric.

Edward considers the situation. He looks at the boy, young, but strong looking.

'Do you want to help us, Eric?' he says.

Eric doesn't say anything, but he places his hare gently on the grass, and climbs down into the trench with the others.

Now it's even more of a squeeze, but they just manage to find a place to stand.

'On three,' says Edward, 'One . . .'

But Eric is already lifting.

My God, thinks Edward, but the boy is strong. He can feel Eric doing most of the lifting, and they follow his lead, as they shift the stone up and then to one side, and slide it onto the grass.

They look.

'Oh my . . .' says Isabella.

'. . . God,' says Nancy.

There are bones in the cist. They are long human bones.

They are somewhat jumbled however, and it takes each of them a moment to realise there is more than one set of bones in the coffin, but it is true, for there below them in the stone box are *two* skulls.

They start to decode what they are seeing.

There is a larger skull, and larger skeleton, and a smaller.

'Are you thinking what I'm thinking?' Nancy asks.

Edward says nothing.

'Yes,' says Mat, simply. 'The larger one is holding the smaller one. That is how it seems to me.'

Eric steps back, picks up his hare, and goes to stand on his new mound again.

He shakes his head, gently.

'Well, so it is,' he says, though no one hears him.

Six

That evening, when they finish work, Edward sends the others back to the Wardhouse without him.

There is something he wants to do.

As they pack up, he notices that Eric has already gone, but he knows where he lives, and he takes a slightly different path out of the meadow, into the lane, and up the steps to Eric's front door.

He knocks and waits.

It's quiet inside, and he wonders if he has made a mistake, but then he hears soft footsteps and the door opens.

A woman stands in front of him. She is about his own age, and has an open, kind face.

'Yes?' she says. Then, 'Oh, I know who you are. You're the archaeologist, aren't you? Speak of the Devil! Eric has been telling me all about you. Won't you come in and have some tea?'

Edward is a little thrown. He can't imagine Eric saying much at all, for one thing.

'I . . . that's very kind. I just wanted to come and thank Eric for his help today. We couldn't have managed without him.'

The woman laughs.

'Think nothing of it. It is I who should be thanking you.

Please, come in and have some tea. We don't get so many visitors.'

Edward finds that surprising, because the woman is lovely. Yes, she's middle aged, as he is, but the lines around her eyes only seem to highlight their elegance. But maybe Eric keeps people away, maybe some people aren't comfortable with someone like . . .

Someone like what?

Edward tells himself off. He's just another human being, he's different, in his own way. Just like everyone. Though he's still surprised that Eric's mother says he's been chatting away about the dig.

'I'm Edward,' he says, holding out his hand.

She shakes it firmly.

'I'm Merle,' she says.

Seven

E ric sits at the table through from the kitchen, playing with his hare. Close to, Edward sees that it is very old; the boy has probably had it since he was a baby. It is tattered and torn, and has obviously been repaired many, many times.

Eric hops the hare across the table one way, then back again, his lips moving wordlessly, as if speaking magic to the toy.

'Yes, I mean it,' Merle says, as she makes tea. 'I can't remember when he was so interested in something. When something made him so happy.'

Happy? thinks Edward.

He doesn't seem particularly happy, but then, maybe he has his own way of showing it. Doesn't everyone?

'He said he helped you lift a big stone . . .?'

'He practically lifted it all by himself. But yes, that's right.'

'He's a strong boy, that's for sure,' she says. 'Well, Eric and I accept your thanks, don't we Eric?'

She calls through to the dining room where Eric sits.

He looks up, briefly, and nods. Then he carries on playing with his hare.

'But that's not really what I came to thank him for.'

'Oh?'

Edward pauses. This is the tricky bit. Where he admits he threw away twenty-six years of professional training because an idiot told him where to dig.

Idiot? He hates himself for even thinking the word. Castigates himself.

He looks through at Eric.

Coughs.

'The thing is . . . the thing is, Merle, that Eric told us where to dig, and we found something amazing. We were having no joy, nothing. Finding nothing, and then Eric told me where to dig this morning, and hey presto! We've hit this incredible find.'

Maybe Merle doesn't understand what he's saying, doesn't get how archaeology works, because she doesn't seem interested in Eric's tip-off.

'What did you find?'

'Viking burial. Not uncommon in itself, but this one is very unusual. I've never seen anything like it before. In fact, I might be going to make my career here. Finally. I don't think anyone's seen anything like it. Ever.'

'Well, then,' says Merle. 'You'll have to thank Eric for that too. Eric? Did you hear that? You've made this nice man famous! Isn't that good?'

'Thanks, Eric!' Edward calls, laughing, but Eric frowns. He gets up from the table, and hurries upstairs.

'Did I upset him?' Edward asks. 'I'm sorry. I . . .'

Merle shakes her head.

'He's hard to understand. Don't worry, he's fine. He's like that sometimes. He's very shy, you see. Very shy.'

Edward wants to ask something, but doesn't know how to say it. But he is genuinely interested in the boy, he likes him, though he barely knows him.

'What . . . I mean,' he says, fumbling for the words, 'Was he . . .?'

'You mean why is he like this?' Merle says. She is not offended. 'Don't worry. I'm actually glad that you asked straight out. Most people beat around the bush, or avoid us altogether.'

'Which is their loss,' Edward says, aloud, before he knows what he's saying.

Merle hesitates. A little light comes into her eyes.

'You're right, Edward, it's their loss.'

She touches his forearm, very gently, very briefly.

'He wasn't born like this. He was born what those *other* kind of people would call normal. It happened when he was two.'

She hesitates again for a moment, remembering.

'It was this time of year. The hay moon. They had started to cut the hay in the meadow, and Eric . . . Eric . . . I couldn't find him. He was here one minute, and I was putting washing out in the garden, and then he was gone. I couldn't find him. I got really desperate, you know. As a parent there's . . . Well, anyway, the next thing was that I heard shouts from the meadow. I ran outside.

'That was where Eric had been. He'd crawled into the hay. It was long, and he must have been hidden. Someone hit him in the grass with a scythe. It didn't cut him, thank God, it hit him on the back swing. It hit him in the head. He was unconscious, we thought he was not going to . . .'

78

She pauses again.

'I'm sorry,' says Edward. 'I shouldn't have asked.'

'No, it's okay. Really. I just haven't told this story in a while. No one is interested, you see.'

'I am,' says Edward, quietly.

Merle mouths the words 'thank you'.

'When he woke up, we knew something was wrong immediately. He was still our little boy, but he had changed. As he grew up, it became more and more obvious.'

'What was he doing in the hay anyway?'

'Who knows? Who knows how a tiny child's mind works? But, well, I've always thought it was because of the hares. Have you seen the hares? On the island?'

Edward shakes his head.

'Well, keep watching, there are lots of them, and Eric was fascinated by them, even when he was tiny. They often sit in the long grass of the meadow, before it's cut. When the scything starts, you can see them bolt for cover somewhere. I think Eric wanted to be a hare, that's all.'

Suddenly Merle grasps Edward's hand earnestly.

'I love him so much. I'd do anything for him, you know? Do you have children, Edward?'

He shakes his head. Thinks about her hand on his.

'I just can't reach him. Not how a mother should. He goes away from me, as if he's on a journey somewhere, somewhere I can't follow. Seeing things I can't see. I can't explain.'

She breaks off, then tries once more.

'It's like loving someone from another world.'

There's a long pause, and then Edward knows there

79

is something else he has to ask, something that has been unspoken but that has been implied in everything since the moment he crossed the threshold into this quiet house, of son, and mother.

'Who did it?'

Merle doesn't reply. She half turns, tilting her head. But Edward cannot let it go.

'Who was it, who hit him with the scythe? I mean it was an accident, of course, but who did it?'

Again Merle pauses a long time before answering.

'It was his father. My husband.'

'Where is he now?' Edward whispers, so quietly he can barely hear his own voice.

Merle's eyes moisten.

'He couldn't cope with what he'd done to our little boy. He's . . . gone.'

Eight

Over supper, the four discuss the find, what it means, how to proceed, but despite the excitement, Edward's mind is only half on the job. The other half of his thoughts are in a house by a meadow, the other half of his thoughts are in that hay meadow, fourteen years ago, as a small boy crawls through the long grass, and curls up to sleep, with his friends, the hares.

The others talk.

'There's an adult and a child, that's clear,' says Mat.

'No, it could be a small woman,' says Isabella. 'And we don't know either sex as yet. Tomorrow, if we lift the skull we should be able to tell something from that. '

'Hip bones are useful too.'

'Sometimes.'

'Well, my guess,' says Nancy, 'is that it's a parent and child. They must have died at the same time, probably disease, and were buried together. The child in the arms of the mother. Or father.'

'That's so sad.'

'It's kind of nice, too, though,' Nancy says. 'It's so protective. As if the parent is keeping their child safe. Even in death. Did you ever read about that Mesolithic burial with the skeleton of a child, lain on a swan's wing? I think that's beautiful too. Like the wing would fly it to heaven.'

Finally Edward snaps out of his trance.

'Well, we know what we know and what we don't know we will learn. Tomorrow, Nancy and Isabella will go on with the bones. Mat and I will continue trench two. There's no room for us in the cist, and we'll only get in your way.'

'Are you sure?' Nancy says.

'Absolutely. But we're going to do it all properly. Which means I have to phone the university in the morning, and that means that in three days, four at the most, many other hands will be here, crawling all over *our* find.'

The three are outraged.

'Come on,' Edward says, 'You know how this works. You're going to have to get used to it. But look at it this way. For the next three days, possibly four, it's all ours, so let's do what we can in the meantime.'

He winks.

ട

They are pleased with their find, but they are unaware that next day they will find something just as remarkable, though it will not be eleven centuries old.

It will be a mere sixty years old, and it is lethal.

Nine

They spend the following day working carefully at the dig, and while Nancy and Isabella begin to lift the bones, Mat and Edward start to make some progress with their trench.

Once more, Eric watches from a mound, clutching his hare tightly.

They've gone really deep now, and have found something that looks like cut wood, not as exciting as the other trench, but possible evidence of settlement, and if the full picture of the cist is to be made clear, they need to build up an impression of the surrounding environment too.

'Should we prop?' Mat asks Edward, mid-morning.

Edward looks at the trench.

'Not yet. No. If we were deeper, or the substrata less coherent, I would say yes.'

Mat doesn't look convinced.

'Are you sure? We've gone much deeper, even this morning.'

Edward knows the boy is right, really; the pit is deep. But they don't have time to go and buy wood on the mainland and make the props and fit them, when all he really wants to do is see what the bones are showing.

'We're okay. We'll press on.'

Mat takes one last look at the ground level, now some way above his head, and back at the ladder which they use to climb into the trench, and then he bends to his work again.

Eric stands sentinel, watching Nancy and Isabella. He has come a little closer today, and holds the hare tightly to his chest, stroking its back from time to time.

The girls lift each bone very, very carefully, as if they are dangerous, because they are so fragile they could shatter at any moment.

As far as they can see, there are no remains of clothing, but there might be microscopic fragments that can be identified in the lab, later.

Then Nancy sees something.

'Hello,' she says. 'What are you?'

Apart from the bones, the grave has seemed bare, but now they have untwined the arms of the man from the arms of the child (as she likes to think of them), and lifted the child's skull and ribs, she has a better view of the adult.

'Something here!' she calls.

Edward doesn't hear, but Mat does.

'They've found something. Shall we go and look?'

'No . . .' says Edward. Then, 'Yes, dammit. Come on.'

'I'll be right there,' Mat says. 'Just finish this.'

Edward climbs out first, up the ladder, and over to the cist. Mat turns to follow, and is half way up the ladder, when something catches his eye.

In the end wall of the trench, behind the ladder, just below the surface, something is poking out of the soil.

He pulls his trowel from his back pocket, and takes a little scrape.

What he sees intrigues him so much, he makes another little scrape. And then a bigger one. He sees metal, and now he carefully digs a whole chunk of soil from the side of the metal.

He realises what he is looking at, and jumps in fright. His feet slip on the damp rungs of the ladder, and he flails at the earth as he falls, dislodging a vast section of the wall, which falls away freakishly.

He shouts, but he's already lying at the bottom of the trench, covered up to his chest in the fall.

Now, almost half exposed, the back end of a bomb hangs above his head.

Ten

A t that moment, Nancy had been about to show Edward what she'd just found in the grave. The spongy, fragile remains of wood among the bones of the adult skeleton.

One part at the chest, the other between the jaws.

They hear Mat's cry, and the tumble of the earth, and from that moment on, everything is blurry.

In a moment, they are at the pit.

At first, they are simply relieved to see that Mat is not fully covered, as they take in the mess of mud, Mat and the ladder. Then they see the horror on his face, as he points wordlessly to the shell, now hanging out of the collapsed wall, right above his head.

'Oh God,' says Edward, in a very small voice.

Then he shouts.

'Go! To Eric's house. His mother can call Emergency. Go!'

The girls run, and Edward edges round to the slightly safer end of the trench.

'Mat. It's going to be okay. They've gone for help. They'll get some help.'

Mat is scared. In shock from the fall, maybe a bone broken too.

'Edward,' he says. 'Edward, Edward . . .'

'Help will come soon,' Edward says, but then he thinks that's probably not true. There's not even a police station on the island, which means sending a boat from the mainland, from Skarpness, which will take at least half an hour.

At that thought, Edward looks up to the far end of the trench, at the bomb, and at the same moment he hears a scream.

The scream is Merle, running across the field.

She's screaming because Eric is kneeling at the trench, by the bomb.

Nancy and Isabella catch up with Merle, and grab her wrists, dragging her backwards, trying to stop her from reaching Eric.

'No! Eric, no!' she wails.

Nancy pulls her back, hard, no longer languid.

Edward looks across the pit at Eric.

There's no way he can rush him, get round to him in time. He thinks quickly, speaks calmly but firmly.

'No, Eric. It's dangerous. Go to your mother, now, Eric. It's dangerous here.'

Mat is lying at the bottom of the hole, fully comprehending the situation.

'Edward, Edward, Edward,' he whimpers, repeatedly.

'Eric. No!'

Eric takes no notice of Edward.

He leans over, and closes his fingers around the tail fin of the rusty shell, dropped by a dive-bomber in the closing stages of the War.

Now, no one dares breathe, even Merle has gone quiet, though she struggles to break free.

At the trench, Eric stands.

The bomb is in his hands.

Edward stands too, his legs turning to water.

Eric looks up at him.

'Eric. It's dangerous.'

By way of reply, Eric stuffs his hare into his jacket pocket, then takes hold of the shell again with both hands.

In the pit, Mat is moaning.

Above it, Edward, Merle, Nancy and Isabella watch as Eric walks across the meadow with the unexploded bomb, heading for the quayside.

In slow motion, they see him climb the steps onto the quay, walk slowly along the stone pier, past all the fishing boats, and stand, a lone figure isolated against the seascape beyond.

He drops the shell into the water, where it slips immediately and quietly out of sight with barely a splash, and calmly Eric turns back to the meadow.

As they run to meet him, and throw their arms around him, he is chewing the ear of his hare.

'It's dangerous, Mummy,' he says.

Merle cries, and cries, and Edward cries too, then pulls himself together. He is responsible here.

'Eric, you are so strong. We need to get Mat out of the hole. Can you do that? Can you help us?'

Eric nods.

Later that day, when everyone has calmed down, they sit around the table in Merle's house.

Mat is fine, just a sprained knee to show for his near premature burial. Everyone is drinking herbal tea, which Merle assures them is the best thing for their nerves.

'It'll help you sleep tonight,' she says. 'You too, Eric. Drink up.'

She comes and stands behind her son, and puts her hands on his shoulders.

'You silly boy,' she says, trying to sound bright. 'You could have been hurt. You could have been killed.'

Eric turns and looks up at his mother.

'No. I couldn't die. I'm not quite the last.'

Nancy and Isabella look at Edward for some explanation. He shakes his head.

'Don't worry about Eric,' Merle explains. 'He sometimes says things that don't really make sense to me.'

'I wouldn't have him any other way,' Edward says, putting his arm around Merle, because it just feels right to.

He's never had children of his own. He thought that time was past, but who knows, he thinks, maybe it's not too late yet.

He knows he'd be proud to call Eric his son, even if he does say strange things, sometimes.

Eric smiles.

'I'm not quite the last,' he says again.

PART THREE

The Airman

August 1944 – The Grain Moon

ॐ

One

———

It is dark when the airman falls from the sky.

Above him, a storm rages, but it is an artificial one; the thunder and lightning are shellfire and tracer bullets.

As he tumbles like a leaf in an autumn gale through the cold night air, he twists gently on his lines, the parachute sighing to him softly from above. He watches the storm, the flashes above him, the flashes below him.

One of those flashes below will be his Supermarine Spitfire, and he tries to still the feeling of fear and loss that this thought gives him. Minutes ago it was a roaring beast, a tiger of the sky, now it will be a bonfire burning around a twelve cylinder Rolls-Royce engine, twisted and broken.

He tries to spot his landing, but it's dark, and the lightning flashes only serve to blind him further.

Then suddenly the ground is right there, and there is no time to prepare himself.

He's unconscious before he even feels the pain.

Two

Hovering between life and death, the airman's dreams are as twisted and broken as his fighter plane, which still smokes on a hillside a mile away. He sees weird visions of heaven and hell, and has a nightmare of running but being unable to run, as something chases him through fiery pits.

He groans in his sleep, and thrashes wildly, disturbing the hare that has been sitting nearby, watching him, wide eyes blinking in the near moonless night. Finally, as he wakes in early daylight, he dreams he's being eaten by a dragon.

He sits up and screams, because his ankle is broken.

A beast scumbles away from him and he sees the dragon from his dreams, a large dog, a wolfhound. He collapses onto his back again, and with his thick leather glove he wipes his face, wet with the dog's slobber.

Turning his neck awkwardly, he sees the lines of his chute stretching across a field of wheat. He's made quite a mess, and suddenly panic takes hold.

He sits up again, this time avoiding using his right leg,

the ankle of which is throbbing in a threatening way.

The dog has run away a few paces, but now sits watching him, panting merrily.

Where the hell am I? he thinks.

The last thing he remembers is that he'd managed to radio Petter before he'd had to bail out, but even then they were way off course, having made a run north to avoid a fighter patrol. What bad luck to hit another one. They'd come from nowhere and taken half the flight down before they even knew what was happening.

They'd been over the coast, God knows where, and he'd seen the lights of a small group of islands, and prayed he'd land on one of them, and not the sea, for to land in the sea would mean death.

He considers the facts, the chances of his survival.

His ankle is broken, he cannot walk.

If his emergency kit has survived, he can inject himself with some morphine, which, while it lasts, will ease the pain.

The island on which he has fallen must be inhabited; this is a wheat field, there is someone's dog.

He knows this is not the mainland, but it could be almost anywhere else; they'd gone a long way north before the dogfight.

He'd radioed Petter, but maybe Petter didn't make it either.

He decides not to think that.

Petter Åkare is a good pilot, and he knows he'll have made it. He'll report their position, and then . . .

Then what?

They're not going to mount a rescue operation for one missing airman, even if he is a flight lieutenant. The best he can hope for is to make contact with friendly forces, get himself picked up by the Navy.

He's just thinking all this when he hears a harsh voice, shouting.

'Skilla! Skilla!'

He fumbles to pull his gloves off.

'Skill-a!'

It's a man's voice, and it sounds angry, even if he doesn't understand what the man is shouting.

He manages to pull his glove off with his teeth, and scrabbles for his pistol, but before he can pop the catch on his holster, the light is blotted out above him by the figure of a man. A large man.

He looks down and whistles.

The dog bounds over to him, begins to lick his hand.

'Well, Skilla,' he says, 'what have you found this time?'

Three

——

'Wait here,' the man says, and the airman is not sure whether he means him or Skilla, because the wolfhound stays, panting noisily beside him, while the man goes.

He is gone a long time, during which the airman wonders if he should try to escape.

'Good idea,' he says aloud to Skilla. 'And where exactly shall I crawl to?'

The dog pants at him some more, hanging out its long pink tongue.

When the man returns, he's with another, younger, man, possibly his son. They have made a stretcher from two spindly pine trunks and some sacking.

Without a word, they cut him free from his lines and lift him on to the stretcher. The pain is almost enough to make him black out once more, but something makes him want to be strong in front of these two quiet men. He bites his lip and focuses on the white clouds floating in the blue sky above him as they carry him out of the wheat field.

Half delirious, he looks at the sky, his real home. That is where I should be, he thinks. In the blue heavens, the engine growling in front of me, the wind whistling behind me. It was why he joined the Air Force, really. If he was going to fight, and if he might be going to die, at least he could fly like an angel first.

That is where I should be. Up there.

But now he is earthbound, and worse than earthbound, for he cannot even walk. He is a worm, stuck to the surface of a ball of mud.

Very soon, the rescue party of silent men and tongue-lolling hound steps across a low wire fence at the edge of the wheat field, and onto a path that winds beside some woods.

They turn down another track, and craning his head to one side, the airman sees they're heading for a farmhouse.

It's very early still. He can't see his watch, but he can tell from the angle of the sun, from the smell of the dew evaporating off the grass, from the morning calls of the cockerels in the farmyard.

A woman runs out of the farmhouse, looks down at him briefly, and nods to the older man.

'Quickly,' she says.

They carry him into the kitchen, set his stretcher on the table, and then lift him off and sit him in a large wooden armchair. He winces as they support his bad leg on a small stool, but he's determined not to fuss.

'Flight Lieutenant D. Thompson, 331st Fighter Squadron,' he says, as smartly as he can, then immediately realises he's being an arse. He's not facing the secret police. Standing looking at him are three farmers, a middle-aged man, his wife, and their son. All three are mystified.

He smiles.

'Call me David,' he says.

The farmer nods.

He looks at his wife.

'This is Rebecka. This is Benjamin. My son.'

He puts a hand on the young man's shoulder. David can't get up but he holds out his hand. The farmer doesn't take it, just stays where he is.

'I am Erik,' he says.

He doesn't smile.

Four

When David wakes again he is in a bed.

He has no idea how long he has slept. After they'd brought him to the farm house, Erik had sent Benjamin back to the wheat field to collect the airman's equipment.

David had told Rebecka how to administer the morphine, and within moments of the injection, he'd started to feel very drowsy, the exhaustion and shock catching up with him

'We will hide your parachute,' Erik said. 'And your equipment.'

But Flight Lieutenant David Thompson was already asleep.

'Well,' said Erik, shaking his head, 'so it is.'

David wakes now in a large but simple room, barely more than a peasant's dwelling. The mattress he's lying on is filled with straw, he's underneath a plain white quilt, stuffed with goose or duck feathers; he can hear both birds in the farmyard.

He might have slept for twenty-four hours, which seems

likely as he's desperate to pee. Which presents a problem, since he cannot walk.

He hears voices downstairs, cannot make out the words, but the voices are raised, arguing.

He hears a door slam, and a few minutes later, footsteps in the corridor. The door opens.

Rebecka puts her head round the door, expecting to find him asleep still.

'Oh!' she says. 'So you are awake, after all.'

'Never felt better,' he lies.

'We thought it best to let you rest for as long as possible.'

'That's very kind. You're very kind, in fact. I don't know how I shall be able to thank you.'

Something passes across Rebecka's face. She comes into the room, and begins fussing and tidying, and he has a chance to appraise her. She has an honest face, he thinks. She is tall, very tall in fact, and strong. The word sturdy pops into his head.

He realises that they have undressed him; all his clothes hang over a chair by the bed neatly. On the top of the pile, even his camouflage pattern silk scarf is precisely folded.

He feels the need again, and coughs.

'I wonder,' he says. 'Call of nature, you know?'

She looks at him blankly, then realises what he means. She reaches under the bed and pulls out a large china pot.

'Do you think you can manage?' she asks.

My God, he thinks in horror, is she offering to help me?

He smiles.

'I'll find a way,' he says briskly.

She leaves, and he performs his task. Every second is agony.

When it is done, he collapses back in bed, beads of sweat forming on his forehead.

I should have got her to give me another jab, he thinks, but very soon he begins to get sleepy again anyway.

As he drifts back to the blue dreaming heavens once more, his eyes fix on his clothes, on the remains of his equipment pack, and he notices something.

His pistol is missing.

Five

When he realises that they have given him their own bedroom, Flight Lieutenant David Thompson insists on being moved to another room, any other room.

There is a long argument, and finally, as he starts to hoist himself out of bed, saying he'll crawl if he has to, they relent.

A while later, he hops down the corridor with Erik on one side and Benjamin on the other. They have to hop sideways as the corridor is so narrow, but very soon he is lifted into a smaller bed in a smaller room.

Now he realises that it's Benjamin's room, and he starts to protest again, especially as they'd passed the closed door of presumably another bedroom on the way down the corridor.

'You are our guest,' Benjamin says, putting his hand on David's forearm. 'And you are ill. It is summer, and I'll be quite well in the barn. The hay has just been cut, last month, and it makes a very soft bed. You should see the hares run as we cut the hay! It's my favourite job. How they run! Crazy!'

The young man prattles on and on, and before long, David has even forgotten what it is they were arguing about.

Rebecka appears in the doorway, with the morphine vial and the needle.

'You are an angel,' David says, for the pain has got worse again, but as he falls asleep, three things worry him.

He has done nothing about finding out where he is.

The pain is still awful, and there is very little morphine left.

And they are arguing again, downstairs. He knows that they are arguing about him.

Six

———

Next day, David feels well enough to get up for a while.

They carry him downstairs and he sits at the kitchen table, in the big armchair, with his foot straight out in front of him, on a cushion on a stool.

Rebecka is cooking at the stove.

Erik and Benjamin have gone out; always working.

David knows how much work there is to do on a farm; when he was a young boy he used to spend his summers in Devon, staying on a farm. He has no idea now, thinking about it, why he went there. His parents were somewhere else. But then, his parents were always somewhere else.

It was while he spent those summers on the farm that he knew he wanted to fly. He can remember, clearly, drinking milk while sitting on the back doorstep of the farmhouse. The milk was still warm from the cow, and as he sat there, it must have been early evening, he guesses, dozens of little birds flew around his head. They were swifts, nesting in cracks in the eaves of the farmhouse.

At that point, he'd never seen a plane, but when he did a year or so later, he knew that's all he wanted to do with his life. That, and fall in love.

Somehow, he knew that when he was a young boy too.

His memories are brought back to the present.

'At least, let me do something,' he says to Rebecka. 'I feel terrible just sitting here, watching you all working.'

Rebecka shrugs, goes to the pantry, and returns with a large basket of peas, still in their pods. Skilla briefly lifts his head from where he sits, under the kitchen table, at David's good foot.

'You can shell these,' she says. 'You know how to do that?'

David can see she's only teasing, but he feels slightly nettled.

'Yes,' he says. 'I know how to do that.'

For a while, they work in silence, David shucking the peas into a white bowl, letting the empty pods lie on the table, and Rebecka chopping and grinding at the stove, where a pot is simmering. There is a strange smell, but David doesn't really notice.

His mind is on other matters.

'Why are you arguing?' he says. 'You're arguing about me, aren't you?'

'No . . .' Rebecka says, but she is interrupted.

'Yes,' says Erik, suddenly filling the doorway. 'We are arguing about you.'

David drops his pea pods and raises a hand.

'Listen. I am very grateful to you both, to you all. But what can I do?'

He looks at his ankle, realising he actually has no idea how long a broken ankle takes to heal.

'You should not have come here,' Erik says, barely hiding his anger.

'I didn't exactly choose to come here,' David says. 'Come to that, I'm not exactly sure where here is.'

'Here,' says Erik, coming into the kitchen, 'is somewhere that is not part of your war. We have not chosen to fight and kill each other. We want to remain out of your war. Neutral. And yet, your war comes here anyway.'

David shakes his head.

'So what would you have me do? I'd like nothing more than to fly away, I promise you that. Just give me my pistol back and I'll be gone.'

Erik grunts, turns and washes his hands in the sink. Drying them, he turns back to David.

'I dropped your gun in the sea,' he says. 'It is part of your war, your life, not ours.'

'What do you mean by "my war"? The enemy . . .'

'The enemy? There are two sides fighting in this war, are there not? But yes, though we said we will not take part, we have *your* enemy on our soil anyway. They should not be here, but there are reports of them all along the coast. And they hunt for the enemy soldiers. For airmen whose aeroplanes have crashed. Just like you. And they will come looking for you, and then your war will come here, to Blest Island.'

He bangs his hand on the table in front of David, so hard that the white bowl wobbles.

He leans down in front of David.

'I want no part of it.'

He turns and storms from the kitchen.

Now angry himself, David calls after him.

'Where is my pistol? What have you done with my pistol?'

But Erik has gone and, cursing his ankle, David cannot follow.

Rebecka stands at the stove still, her back to the scene, her shoulders trembling.

Seven

The days pass.

With each day, David's ankle is healing.

The morphine has run out, but in its place, Rebecka has been feeding him a constant supply of a special black tea. Every day she chops and grinds at the stove, concocting that rather strange smelling liquid in a small pot.

Although it smells unpleasant, David has to concede that the tea more than takes the edge off the pain.

'It's something my mother used to make us when we were ill,' Rebecka explains. 'And her mother taught her, before that. We have this very special flower here, it only grows on the western half of the island. Nobody knows why but it will not grow on this side. Look.'

She holds up a very bizarre looking flower. It is purple-black. He thinks it looks like a dragon's head.

'It can work miracles, you know, if prepared properly,' she says.

He even wonders if it is helping his ankle to heal faster, for after a couple of weeks, he can hobble slowly down the corridor, and even get downstairs, though that hurts a lot.

The days pass.

They give David some old clothes of Erik's to wear. Just to be on the safe side. They are big for him, and he feels silly. And more than that, it's odd to wear another man's clothes, especially when that man seems to hate you. But it makes sense.

'Maybe Benjamin is more your size,' Rebecka says, looking him up and down. At that moment Benjamin walks into the kitchen.

'Well,' says Rebecka, 'Speak of the Devil and his horns appear. What do you think, should we give David some of your clothes instead?'

'I think he looks just fine as he is,' says Benjamin solemnly, and then bursts out laughing.

Rebecka chases him off, batting at his head with a large wooden spoon.

The days pass.

David gets better, but the mood in the house gets worse.

The arguments continue, David can hear them at night, along the corridor from his room. He knows he needs to do something, but he has no idea what. When he can walk, he can just walk away, even if it means walking into captivity. Or worse.

Over mealtimes, no one speaks.

Even Skilla is quiet, lurking in the shadows under the table.

Eventually, David can stand the atmosphere no longer, and after they have finished their evening meal of chicken stew and black bread, with great effort, he stands up.

He looks at the three whose lives he is endangering.

'Throw me out,' he says. 'I can't bear this, and I can't be responsible for your safety. Put me in a cart and drop me back in the fields somewhere. I'll fight my way out of this. I've done it before.'

He has done no such thing, but it makes him feel brave to say it.

No one says anything, then finally, Erik clears his throat.

'Sit down, David Thompson,' he says.

Then Erik gets up, and leaves.

'Benjamin, help your mother,' he says, as he goes. 'I have work to do.'

Rebecka puts her hand on Benjamin's shoulder.

'Go with your father,' she says, 'I can manage here.'

When the men are gone, David sits again. He does so with great relief – he is almost weeping from the pain of standing on his ankle.

'What is it?' he asks, when he gets his breath again.

'What do you mean?'

'It's not just this war. This war that you say you are not a part of. You may not want to be a part of the war, but you are part of the world. And the world is at war. It's not a question of what you want.'

Rebecka says nothing. She clears up for a while, then

111

turns to look at David, dish-cloth in hand, leaning back against the sink.

'Erik says . . .'

'What? That I am dangerous? That I will get you into trouble? He might be right, you know. Maybe you should listen to your husband. Throw me out before soldiers come looking for me.'

'No one knows you are here.'

'Are you sure? What about the other villagers? Did no one see me arrive? Is no one wondering why Benjamin is sleeping in the barn on sacks of grain?'

Rebecka doesn't answer that.

'He is not a bad man,' she says instead, quietly.

'I never said he was.'

'But you are right. It is not just the war. None of us want the war, but, you are right, there is something else.'

David feels the tension in her voice, and feels his own heart beating. He knows what she is about to say.

'You may have seen there is an empty room upstairs . . .'

She stops, puts a hand to her mouth, shakes her head, and clears her throat.

'Benjamin is – was – not our only child. We had a daughter too. Her name was Sarah. She was twelve years old. One day, two summers ago, planes flew overhead. They were being chased by your people. They were fighting.'

Her voice lowers a little, but she presses on.

'We were out in the fields, we ran for cover. Then the planes dropped their bombs. Benjamin says they only did it to be lighter, so they could fly faster, and escape. He has read about it. And they did escape, but they let their bombs fall on the island first.'

Rebecka's voice is a whisper now – David's own heartbeat is louder than her words.

'Sarah was at the farm. She ran to the woodsheds. One of the bombs fell right there.'

She turns back to the sink, wringing the dish-cloth.

'That is why Erik is so angry. This war, that none of us want, took our girl away from us. What had she done? Why her?'

She looks David in the eye, tears running down her face.

She whispers.

'Why?'

Eight

The days on the farm pass, as if no war had ever existed. Erik and Benjamin work endless hours in the fields, Rebecka runs the house and the farmyard.

They are indefatigable, tireless, stoic, and given the tragedy of their daughter, David decides, they are still people with life inside them.

Only once does he hear anything like a complaint.

'There's much to do,' Rebecka tells him one afternoon, as she makes his special tea. 'Always so much to do on a farm, but nothing compared to when we harvest the wheat. That's when the work really starts.'

Even then, David detects no self-pity in what she says. It is simply their life here, on the island, on the farm.

'When do you cut the grain?' David asks. He is struck by a desire to help. If it's not too soon, his ankle might be better enough.

'After the grain moon.'

'The grain moon? What's that?'

'Just what it says. We still use the old names for the moons here, the full moons. They come from the land, from life on the land. Calf moon, when the animals give birth, leaf moon, when the leaves return to the trees. The flower moon. Grain moon.'

David nods, thoughtfully.

'I like those,' he says. 'I like those a lot. And when is the grain moon?'

'The day after tomorrow,' Rebecka says, and David knows then he won't be able to help.

Nine

Until that moment when Rebecka told him about the death of their daughter, David had not thought of home.

Unconsciously, he'd decided to suppress such thoughts, as they would have hurt far more than his ankle ever could.

David sits alone at the kitchen table, staring out of the window. Vaguely he notices smoke from a bonfire in the farmyard, then he hears shouting outside.

They are arguing again, but this time Benjamin is involved too.

Suddenly, Benjamin is back in the kitchen.

'Mr Thompson,' he says breathlessly, 'my father is burning your things.'

David almost jumps from the chair.

'What?' he cries. 'What? Why?'

'I don't know. He won't make sense.'

'I must stop him. Will you help me?'

Benjamin nods and becomes a crutch on David's right side. Together, they hobble out of the kitchen and into the farmyard, where Erik has an old oil drum with the end cut off. Grey smoke broils from inside, in thick choking clouds.

David is too late, Erik is poking the last of David's uniform into the drum with a hefty wooden stick.

Skilla runs around, barking.

David's heart is pounding.

'What on earth are you doing? What gives you the right to do that? Stop it!'

Without waiting, and heedless of the pain in his ankle, he lunges at the barrel, knocking it flying, and sending smoke and spits of fire across the mud of the yard. He sees what he feared was in there, and grabs his smouldering flying jacket.

Sinking to his knees, he bats at the burning leather, frantically hunting through the pockets.

'Right?' shouts Erik. 'It is not a question of right. It is a question of sense. There are soldiers coming. I heard it in the village today. They have been on the other islands, to the south, hunting for men like you.'

David hears him but ignores him, and ignores the burns he's inflicting on himself, as he turns his jacket inside out, searching for something as if his life depends on it.

Finally, he finds what he is looking for, drops the jacket on the ground, and sits back, speechless.

It had seemed so unreal here, like a dream, in this little idyllic haven, away from the war. But Erik was right after all. The war has come back to find him, to the very doorstep of the island.

Soldiers are coming.

'And if they come here, there must be no trace,' Erik says. 'Of you.'

He sets the barrel upright again, and with the stick fishes everything back off the ground and inside.

He pulls matches from his pocket and sets it all alight again, and this time, David makes no effort to stop him.

He sits on the ground, clutching something tightly to his chest.

He is trembling.

'What do you have there?' Erik asks roughly. 'Everything of yours must be burned.'

David does not answer.

'Do you hear me?' shouts Erik. 'Everything!'

He makes to grab at whatever is in David's hands, but David pulls away and they begin to fight, wrestling on the ground.

'No!' screams Rebecka. 'Stop it!'

Benjamin loiters, unsure what to do. Skilla barks.

'No,' cries Rebecka again.

The men do not listen to her, but it is over soon. Erik is stronger than David, and the airman is injured after all.

Erik stands, grimly about to cast the object into the flames when he stops.

He looks at it.

It is a wallet, a simple one that folds in half.

Erik opens it, looks for a long time, then slowly closes it again.

He holds it in the air for a moment, his arm out-stretched, as if thinking, and then he drops it at David's feet, and walks away, into the farmhouse.

Rebecka approaches. She sees what her husband saw.

The wallet has flopped open, and inside is a photograph.

She kneels beside David, who picks the wallet up and shows her the photograph.

It's a portrait, of three people. One of them is David, in his uniform. He has his arm around a pretty woman; his wife. Standing in front of them, her head tilted to one side, and a smile on her face, is their daughter.

Rebecka takes the photograph and David lets her.

'What is her name?' she asks quietly.

'My daughter?' David asks.

She nods.

'Merle. Her name is Merle.'

Ten

That night, David goes to bed early.

He's been drinking Rebecka's tea like water, and it really appears to be working miracles on his ankle, as well as making him very sleepy.

He is getting ready for bed, when there is a knock at the door.

'Yes?' he calls.

Rebecka comes in, and behind her, Benjamin.

They both look solemn.

As David climbs into bed, they each stand at one corner of its foot. Rebecka twists her hands nervously.

'Benjamin,' she says. 'Tell David what you heard.'

Benjamin nods.

'I was in the village today, at the inn, and there I spoke to a fisherman called Stefan. Stefan was in Skarpness yesterday and he heard talk in the harbour there.'

He pauses.

'Go on, Benjamin,' says Rebecka, but Benjamin seems scared, as if what he has to say is risky. And maybe it is.

Rebecka helps him out.

'We may not be fighting in this war, David, but some of our people don't like having foreign soldiers telling us what to do. There is a resistance movement, and they have made contact with your people. It seems they know you are here somewhere. They have come for you, and have put word around that if you are able to travel, you should present yourself at the tavern in Skarpness, on the docks.'

David is speechless.

Petter made it home.

Somehow, this single, wonderful piece of news is enough to make him dissolve in tears. He buries his face in his hands, and Rebecka nods at Benjamin to leave. When David raises his head again, they are alone.

'But, what can I do? How can I get there?'

'You will take our rowing boat. Tomorrow night. It will be too dangerous by day, but the moon is full tomorrow, the grain moon. It will be bright, and you will see the lights of Skarpness to guide your way.

'Go to the tavern in the docks. Ask for a man called Lindberg. He works there. I know him. But I didn't know he works for the resistance.'

'But your boat . . .? Erik?'

'Erik has said you are to take the boat.'

Eleven

The following day is over in a moment, and yet seems to last for centuries.

Every ten minutes, David finds himself checking the height of the sun in the sky, waiting for dusk, but this far north, it has gone nine o'clock before the sun finally disappears behind the western hill of the island.

All day, Rebecka fusses, making food for his short journey, strapping his ankle tightly, then unstrapping it, then strapping it once more. She feeds him lots of tea, tells him to keep all weight off his leg until he has to.

Benjamin loiters in the yard with Skilla, not coming close, unable to pull away.

Erik is nowhere to be seen.

Finally, at ten o'clock, as David sits in the kitchen, getting his last instructions from Rebecka, Erik walks back into the house.

'Well,' he says. His voice is flat, his face is expressionless. He looks at David. 'It's time. Everything's ready.'

David stands, and winces, but in truth, he can walk now.

There is silence, as the two men contemplate each other, yet say nothing.

Rebecka slides a packet of food into a knapsack, and hands it to David.

He is about to thank her, when Benjamin blunders into the kitchen.

'There are soldiers! Here! In the village!'

His eyes are wild, and his panic infects them all.

'In the village? Are you sure?'

'Gregor saw them, and cycled to tell us. They're coming this way!'

'You must go,' cries Rebecka. 'Hurry, hurry!'

Now there is no time for goodbyes. David throws his arms briefly around Rebecka, and Benjamin, who stands in the doorway of the farmhouse. Then Erik hurries away into the moonlit night, David hobbling at his side.

They take a small lane, one that rises over a hill, and down through some woods, to an empty field.

At the end of the field, David can already hear the sea, and a narrow path leads to a dilapidated jetty.

They hurry, but David is struggling. Not only does his ankle hurt, he's had no exercise for several weeks.

Suddenly there are shouts on the lane behind them. Torchlight.

'They're here,' Erik whispers. 'Quick, we'll hide in the boathouse.'

They duck the last few steps, through a low doorway,

into the boathouse, where Erik's boat is moored. It bobs in the water, waiting to be off.

'We'll be safe here,' hisses Erik. 'Until they've gone. They won't think to look here. Maybe.'

David nods in the darkness, in pain again.

'All right,' he says. 'All right.'

They wait, and the voices they heard soon fade. They wait some more.

Erik points at the moonlight shining across the water.

'The moon is bright,' he says. 'You should have no trouble seeing. When this moon is over, we cut the wheat, on the next dry day. I think we'll be cutting wheat tomorrow.'

David nods.

'I wish I could be here to help you.'

He means it. It would be one small way of repaying them, in return for what they've done.

'I think it is nearly time for you to go,' Erik says, and he helps David into the boat.

Suddenly, they hear voices again. Close.

Very close.

Erik swears.

'Go,' he hisses.

'I'll be a sitting duck if they see me!' David hisses back.

Erik says nothing. When he speaks again, his words seem idiotically inappropriate.

'Your daughter,' he says. 'Your daughter. How old is she?'

David desperately looks at the shore line, beyond the boathouse. Any moment he expects to see soldiers silhouetted against the starry sky. The voices are coming closer.

'She's twelve. Twelve.'

Erik nods.

'I thought so,' he says. 'I could tell. I knew it . . . Just like our Sarah.'

He pushes the prow of the boat, silently, yet hard and strong, and as he does so, he leans over and drops something heavy in David's lap.

'Just in case of trouble,' Erik whispers.

The shouts are right behind the shed. If they come round the side, David will be seen, and it will all be over.

Erik stands, and being careful to make noise, he begins to run along the shoreline, the opposite way, away from David and the boat, calling out as he goes.

David picks up the oars, and begins to row, as powerfully but as quietly as he can. Very soon he is out to sea, and safe. He ships the oars, and feels for what Erik dropped in his lap.

It is his service pistol that he thought had been thrown away.

In the pure bright moonlight, he half sees Erik, a shadow moving along the coast. The soldiers are after him, running.

Torchlight sweeps the dark, and finds Erik.

There is a short sudden clatter of machine gun fire.

It stops.

David knows that Erik will not be cutting the wheat tomorrow.

Twelve

David Thompson's daughter Merle has a favourite story, one that she never forgets as she grows up, about how a man called Erik, who she never met, saved her father, and gave him back to her. What she is never told is what really happened to Erik; that is a secret that David and Esmé, his wife, keep to themselves. It would only hurt the child to know it, they think, and anyway, they are grateful enough for all three of them, as the first years pass.

Esmé dies at the age of sixty-three, and even Merle dies before her father, at seventy.

David Thompson himself lives to be one hundred and one years old.

His life is a happy life, and he remains physically fit, and fairly sharp right up to the end, as if he once drank some elixir of life.

In fact the only thing that ever ails him is arthritis in that dodgy ankle.

Eventually, a short but fatal pneumonia takes him.

Even on the morning of the day he dies, however, he still reads his paper over breakfast, from cover to cover. On this particular day, he reads about a startling discovery of a Viking burial, on a small island in the north.

He's always been interested in archaeology, but it's something else about this story that tickles at his memory.

Something about the island, though he can't remember exactly what.

He thinks he might have been there, once, a lifetime ago.

PART FOUR

The Painter

———

September 1902 – The Fruit Moon

৬

One

———

On the girl's seventh birthday, her finest present was not the new white smock, nor the carved wooden hare, though she loved those two things very much.

The best thing was not a thing at all, but a permission.

Mother faced daughter across their small kitchen floor.

The girl tilted her head on one side.

'Merle, it is your seventh birthday today, and seven years ago, when you were born under a bright fruit moon, I did not think you would grow up so fast. But you have.'

Merle nodded solemnly.

'So you have, so I think you are ready, now, to come with me.'

Merle squeaked and jumped into the air.

'Really?' she said.

'Yes, unless I have made the wrong decision and you are not yet sensible enough to come with me?'

Merle stood rooted to the spot and put a serious face on.

'Yes, Mother.'

'Very good. Then tomorrow we will both go to the western isle.'

Merle slept with her new smock bundled up under her head, instead of her pillow. In her hand she clutched the carved running hare, its long ears sleeked along its back, under her tight fingers.

But it was not hares she dreamed of. It was dragons.

Two

———

'Why does no one live here?'

Merle was always full of questions. Their house was a small one on the steep hill up out of the centre of Blest Island, the very path that led to the western half.

Theirs was the last on the right before the top, which meant that Bridget, Merle's mother, could come and go unseen to the western half.

This was good, because though many people on the island made use of her skills and her preparations, there were others who disapproved of what she did. In days gone by, she knew, her art had been normal, welcomed, supported, but it seemed those days were gone.

The modern world had arrived with the new century, and Bridget read about it sometimes; the amazing new things that science had created: of lighter-than-air ships, of pocket cameras, of wireless transmissions.

She didn't object to such things, she just didn't understand why the old things she had learned from her mother should be swept aside by the new. And there lay a problem, because even Merle herself didn't understand fully the ways of the dragon flower plant, that could heal if prepared in a certain way, or could kill if prepared in another. She had learned a little of its ways, but no one knew everything about it any more, of all the uses it could be put to, of all the dangers it held.

'I didn't say no one lives here,' she told Merle.

'But no one comes past our house and we live at the end of the lane.'

Bridget smiled. What a clever young daughter I have.

'In the old days, more people used to live on the western side. But they moved away. I don't know why, but I'm glad. Only Nature lives there now. That's all. Well, almost all.'

Merle didn't hear this last part, because having got to the top of the hill, she raced down the long slope on the far side, her arms stretched out to each side as if to gather the fading September light.

'Wait for me at the bottom!' her mother cried. 'Remember! There are dragons there!'

Merle squealed with delight.

Three

———

They walked across the scrubby terrain of the western half, rocks and grasses, heather and marshes; the soil squelching underfoot in places, like walking on sponge.

'Have you seen the dragons yet?' Bridget asked her daughter.

Merle shook her head, then looked around searchingly.

'Yes!' she cried. 'There! Is that one? Yes! And there! And there!'

Suddenly, she was seeing the flowers on all sides.

'Which ones do we cut?' she asked.

'As many as we can,' said Bridget, putting two well-used wicker baskets on the ground beside them. 'They won't flower for much longer, and we can dry some and boil the rest. Here . . .'

From her pocket she pulled out a folding clasp knife, and handed it to Merle.

'It's not a toy, Merle. It's very sharp. Always cut away from you. Let me show you first.'

Merle took the knife and held it very carefully.

She knelt beside her mother as Bridget sliced one of the Dragon Orchids through its stem, quite near the base.

'There, you see? Like that. Away from you. Right, you try.'

Merle copied just what her mother did, and her mother smiled.

'Very good. But you can take a bit more of the stem. We can make different things from the stems. And from the roots, too, but they're different again, do different things, and I don't like to work with them.'

'Why not, Mummy? Are they poisonous?'

Bridget considered this.

'Yes,' she said, 'in a way.'

Merle listened, nodded.

They cut flowers for an hour or so, then Bridget stood, stretching her back.

'I'm stiff,' she said. 'Ow.'

'Poor Mummy,' said Merle, and then copied her mother, arching her back and sighing deeply. 'Poor Merle. Ow.'

They set off for home, taking a different way back.

'I always prefer a walk that goes in a circle,' Bridget explained to her daughter. 'Don't you?'

Merle hadn't thought about this before.

'I don't know. I think I like there-and-back walks too.'

As they came back to their starting point, Merle suddenly stopped.

'I thought you said no one lived here,' she said.

'No, you weren't listening. I said *almost* no one lives here.'

'So who lives there?' said Merle, pointing at the huge building she had glimpsed through the trees.

The building was more like a church than a house, a single storey of one massive pitched roof, with a tower of some sort on the end forming an impressive entrance way.

Merle's eyes were wide.

'Who lives there, Mummy?'

'A dragon,' said Bridget. 'So just you stay away, because he eats small girls for his lunch.'

Merle squealed. They both ran, and got half way up the hill home before they were too tired to run any more.

At bedtime, Bridget tucked Merle under the sheets, but Merle still had more questions.

'Mummy?' she asked. 'I don't think it can really be a dragon who lives in that big house. So who does live there?'

Bridget smiled.

'He's nearly a dragon,' she said. 'He's an old man, and he's not very friendly. I don't want you going there, all right?'

Merle nodded.

'But who is he?'

'He's an old man. That's all. He's a painter, or at least, he was. That's what they say. And he's very rich. Once he was the most famous painter in the whole land, but then something happened, and they say he hasn't painted anything in years. After that he moved here, and had that house built, like a church all of his own. And I don't want you going there. Now you sleep well and dream of your hare, yes?'

Merle nodded.

She closed her eyes and gripped her hare tight, but she already knew she was going to go the painter's house, just for a look.

Four

―――――

The very next day, Merle took her chance.

Bridget was busy in the kitchen with the flowers they had cut the day before.

'I don't think you're old enough to help with this part, yet,' she'd said to Merle, who had done her best to look sad about it, but was actually secretly glad.

'Don't worry. I'll go into the village and find someone to play with.'

Bridget nodded, distracted. There was a lot of preparation to do – they had picked more flowers than she realised and they needed to be cut and prepared today before their potency went. Then she would have to split and hang all the stems – pounding them would have to wait for another day.

'Be back for lunch,' Bridget said.

'When's that?'

'When your tummy rumbles.'

Merle skipped out of the door and down the hill, then into a neighbour's garden, crawled past the vegetable patch right underneath the kitchen window, and in two minutes was back on the lane to the western side.

'I'm going to see a dragon, I'm going to see a dragon,' she sang as she went.

At the bottom of the hill, she nearly forgot which path

to take, but then she remembered they'd done a circle walk and not a there-and-back walk.

She set off to her left, and in two minutes there was the house again.

She stopped, listening for the sounds of the dragon sleeping, or snoring. Or eating small children; crunching on their bones. She shivered at the thought.

She was just wondering whether dragons only eat girls, and not boys, given the choice, when she saw the orchard.

To the side of the house sat a beautiful orchard of apple trees, and some pear trees. The grass of the orchard was overgrown, almost touching the boughs in places. Here and there enormous weighty clusters of mistletoe, Baldur's bane, clung to the treetops.

The orchard was heavy, ripe and bursting to deliver. Merle's mouth hung open – she had never seen trees with so much fruit on them before. They hung with clusters of apples, their branches pulled low by the weight.

And though her tummy was not actually rumbling yet, she thought it might be a good idea to have an apple anyway, so that she could stay out for a bit longer than she otherwise might.

She looked at the house.

She could see no windows on the side that faced her, the front. Rather it had some kind of long gallery that ran around at head height, and there were windows in this gallery. But she could not see into the house itself, and neither could she hear anyone.

She walked up the path that led to the house, as quietly as she could, and then stopped again.

Still nothing.

She stepped off the path and went around the side of the house, walking through a gate that was so old and rickety that it had fallen off its hinges. She liked that, it made her feel less as though she was trespassing than if she'd had to open the gate.

There were apples on the ground already, many windfalls that lay rotting in the long uncut grass. But there were many, many more still in the trees, and she crept forward, reaching up her hand and sliding her fingers round one that was particularly red and lovely.

As she did so, there was a shout from behind her.

'Hey!'

She turned to see the dragon.

He was on the gallery that ran round this side of the house too, and was waving a small stick at her.

He was angry, really angry.

'Hey you! Get away from there! Go away!'

His voice was broken with anger and age, and terrified, Merle ran as fast as she could, tears already in her eyes.

It was only when she stopped running, half way up the hill to home again, that she realised she had the apple in her hand.

She bit it.

It was delicious.

She sat on a rock on the Outlook, looking to the sea, and finished it, and by the time she had, her tears were finished too.

In fact, she felt really happy.

She bounded in to the kitchen.

'Hello, Mummy, is it lunchtime yet?'

Five

Next day, all day Merle fussed and fretted, trying not to go back to the orchard. Finally Bridget snapped at her.

'What is wrong with you? Get out from under my feet! I have all these stems to pound, and the first lot of flowers need to come out of the pot. So be off!'

Merle took that as a sign, if not actually an order, to go back to the orchard.

She stood for a long time at the end of the path, waiting.

Hearing nothing, seeing no one, she set off up the path and around the side to the orchard gate.

She waited again.

It seems such a shame, she thought to herself.

Such a shame, that here are all these apples and pears going to waste, and no one picking them and them all falling on the grass and going nasty, with only the worms and maggots to enjoy them.

So that she wouldn't be seen from the house, she got down on her hands and knees and crawled through the orchard, pretending she was an animal, her hare maybe.

Hares always moved silently, rarely seen, she knew that.

She sat in the long grass, and found a windfall that the worms hadn't yet, and as she chewed its sweet flesh, she began to think about the dragon.

He wasn't a dragon really, she knew that. He was just an old man. She knew that her mother had explained that some old people in the village found it hard to do things. Or that sometimes they found it hard to hear, and that could make it seem like they were rude, when really they weren't.

Suddenly, it occurred to Merle that maybe the old man wasn't picking his apples, because he couldn't.

She'd only had a brief glimpse of him, but he did seem very old, and his shoulders were hunched.

That seemed sad to Merle, and she thought that he'd probably love to have an apple, if only he could pick one.

She ran into the orchard.

She picked two apples.

She ran as fast as she could to the front door step, left one apple there, and then ran home, saving the other to eat on her rock at the top of the hill.

Six

Whe Merle went back the day after, she smiled.
The apple had gone, and she knew she was right.
He did want them after all.

ॐ

She slipped into the orchard once more, though still checking first to see that he was not around.

She picked four apples this time, and left two on the doorstep.

She ate an apple on the rock at the top of the hill, and sneaked the other into her bedroom, in case she was hungry in the night.

At bedtime, she kissed her hare on the nose, and went to sleep.

She dreamed of flying on the back of a dragon, right above the island, right over her house. She looked down at her house and saw her mother in the back garden, looking up and waving, and smiling.

Seven

On the next day, she waited until the afternoon, and picked six apples.

She put three on the doorstep, and brought the others home, eating one on her rock, and sneaking two into her bedroom.

At supper time, her mother seemed tired. She had been working so hard on the flowers and the stems for three days.

Merle wanted to give her one of her apples. She always felt so much better after eating them, but she knew that if she did she would have to say where it came from, so she didn't.

'Merle,' said Bridget, 'you haven't been to the western side without me, have you? To the old man's house?'

Merle shook her head.

'You won't do that, will you? It might seem tempting, but you mustn't. Do you understand?'

'Yes, Mummy,' said Merle. She felt bad about lying, but she would confess it to her hare at bedtime and that would make it better.

Next day, when she went back to the western side, she had not even got up the path before she realised that the three apples she had left the day before were still there.

'That's not right,' she said.

She walked up to the house, and for some reason, she didn't feel afraid.

There were the three apples from the day before, sitting where she'd left them.

Not right.

She stood at the front door, an absolutely tiny figure against its vast size. She stretched up one tiny hand and knocked.

It made almost no sound, so she tried again, as hard as she could.

Now she was sure that the old man must have heard her, so she waited, and waited for something to happen, but nothing did.

She tried to open the door then, but although she could just reach the handle, the door seemed to be locked.

'That's odd,' she said.

She looked to her left.

There was the gallery, that ran round the house, and she decided to see if there was another way in.

She turned the corner, feeling the wood of the balustrade under her hand, slightly peeling light blue paint, the lovely smell of warm wood, and then there was the orchard below her, and then, there . . . there was a door.

It was open, and Merle knew she would have to go into the dragon's lair.

Timidly, like a hare, she stuck her head round the corner of the door.

It took her a moment to see.

It was so dark inside, with very few windows, and her eyes took a while to adjust.

It was a huge room, more a space than a room, like the inside of a church. At first she saw nothing, but then she heard a faint noise from some way inside.

Then she saw him.

'Oh!' she cried.

He was lying on the floor, on his side.

At her shriek, he opened his eyes.

Merle thought he seemed confused.

'Oh,' she said again. 'Are you all right? Why are you lying on the floor? Can't you get up?'

The old man's eyes focused on her now.

He opened his mouth to speak, but no words came out.

Then he simply shook his head.

'Wait there!' cried Merle, 'I'll get Mummy!'

She ran, ran fast, and all the way up the hill, and didn't stop till she burst in through the kitchen door.

'It's the dragon man,' she cried. 'He's ill!'

Eight

Bridget thought there was nothing seriously wrong with the old man, he'd had a fall and hadn't been able to get up, that was all.

She'd sent Merle home for some of her special tea, and while her daughter was gone, Bridget picked him up and set him on a sofa at the edge of the big room.

She looked about her.

'Do you have a kitchen?' she asked.

There was no way of knowing where such a thing might be – this was not a normal sort of home.

The old man nodded, and she set off.

The kitchen was small, and primitive. She hunted through the cupboards, and found very little. Some flour, some biscuits. Some sour milk.

On the worktop sat a couple of apples.

Merle bustled back into the kitchen, and handed Bridget the tea, then she went to sit with the old man while her mother brewed a pot.

'Drink this,' she said. 'I've put some cold water in it, so it isn't too hot.'

The old man took the tea, still without words, and drank, drank the whole thing down, in one go.

He handed the cup back to Bridget, closed his eyes,

briefly, and then lifted his head.

He held out his hand to Bridget.

'Eric Carlsson,' he said. 'Thank you.'

Bridget recognised his name.

'Mummy?' asked Merle. 'What's that?'

Bridget turned to see Merle standing, looking at the far end of the room, and now she finally saw it too.

The painting.

A vast, vast painting.

Bridget was drawn to it, her feet carrying her towards it without her thinking. Her mouth hung open, she had never seen anything like it, anything so mysterious, so compelling, so terrifying.

Merle trotted over to stand next to her, looking at the painting too.

Around about, on the floor, stood another easel, with a sketch on it. Tables and tables of oil paints, pallet knives, brushes and turpentine stood next to the easel. The painting seemed almost finished, but Bridget could see there were a few areas still left to be completed.

It was work in progress, and the progress must have taken a very long time already.

'What is it, Mummy?' she asked.

Bridget did not answer.

How could she explain what she saw to such a young child?

She remembered about Eric Carlsson. It was true, he had been the most famous painter of the last century. Born in a poor quarter, he had begun his career in the city, where he made a living drawing quick sketch portraits on the street, until some rich patron had spotted his talent and paid for him to go to art school. He'd made a name for himself then, painting portraits that seemed more alive than the subjects themselves, so they said.

His reputation grew, but he started to make real money when he began a series of paintings of family life. He had moved to the countryside with his wife and family, where he painted modest, charming depictions of everyday life in the old-fashioned way: summer dances, evening songs by the piano, butter churning, Christmas celebrations.

His paintings were reproduced, and sold, and he became very, very rich.

Bridget remembered those paintings, in fact, she even thought she had one of them somewhere in their own house, but the thing she was looking at came from somewhere else, from another time, from another world, from another dimension even.

⟲

For a start, the painting was big. Many of the people depicted were more than life-size, and she counted over thirty before she lost track.

It showed some kind of ritual, some terrible act. Then, she realised, what it actually showed was the moment *just before* some terrible act took place.

At the back of the painting was a building, a building she recognised as the one in which they were standing. Various figures crowded the galleries, watching the scene unfold below.

There were about twenty more people in the foreground.

On the left were a group of women in traditional dress, dancing, fingers intertwined above their heads. The music to which they danced came from five musicians, dressed like priests of some sort. Two played long curling horns, of a kind which Bridget had never seen before, the other three played long straight horns, blasting their primal notes up into the sky. In front of the musicians, two more figures, men dressed in furs and leather, danced crazy contorted shapes, as if in pain, their eyes staring and wide.

Behind them grew a tree, an odd tree, with a straight trunk, and a pointed crown of brilliant green leaves. Gold objects hung in the glossy leaves, and Bridget was startled as she saw that they were skulls. Shining golden skulls.

To the right were the warriors, half a dozen or more, carrying long spears, dressed in ceremonial robes, with proud helms upon which sat totemic figurines: a fox, a boar, a raven. A hare.

But it was the centre of the painting that disturbed the most.

Here were the three main players.

The first was a priest, the high-priest maybe, with a white beard, and blind in one eye. In his hands he gripped a ceremonial golden hammer.

Second, was the king. Bridget knew he was the king because he wore a crown, but, oddly, shockingly, he was naked. At that very moment, he had let fall a rich fox fur robe, even now it slipped from his right shoulder to the ground, as he was carried forward to the centre of the painting on a shining sleigh, again covered in gold.

And then there was the third figure.

Seen from behind, his head bowed, was a figure robed all in red. Blood red.

Tucked behind his right forearm, out of sight of the king, the figure in red held a long and deadly knife.

He was the executioner.

His moment had come.

The king lifted his bearded jaw to the heavens, his eyes rolling back in his head.

He knew his moment had come, too.

Nine

Bridget and Merle walked home.

'Merle,' said her mother. 'You have been naughty.'

Merle had been waiting for this.

'I know.'

'You lied to me and that is very bad.'

They stopped walking, Bridget looked down at her daughter.

'I'm sorry, Mummy,' said Merle.

'Very well,' said Bridget. 'We will say no more of it. Anyway, I knew you were lying to me, because I found apples in your bedroom.'

Merle blushed.

'I'm sorry,' she repeated.

'But I want to say something else,' Bridget said. 'What you did today was good, and very brave. You might have saved the old man's life.'

'He's called Eric Carlsson,' said Merle, suddenly bright again. 'He's a painter.'

Bridget nodded, and smiled.

'He certainly is that,' she said. 'But listen, I think he needs our help, just for a while. So we're going to make him a hot meal every day, and you can pick him a few apples every day too. Would you like that?'

Merle nodded happily, her hair fell across her eyes.

'But we'll do it together, and you must promise me you won't go on your own again. Yes?'

'Yes,' said Merle. And she felt happier, because this time she knew she meant it.

Ten

———

Every day, they took Eric some food, and while Bridget tried to make sense of the kitchen, Merle sat and talked to the old painter.

Bridget was amazed what they found to talk about, the young girl and the old man, but talk they did, while she tidied and cleaned and swept in the cavernous building that Eric had made his home.

Often, when she came into the room where they sat, the conversation would falter a little; when she left, she'd hear them chatting away again. She didn't mind. She was pleased that her daughter had a friend, even if he was ten times her age, and she was pleased for the old man too.

Bridget eavesdropped on their chatter one day, as she swept the early fallen leaves from the gallery right outside the painting room, as she called it. It was as if Eric was the child and Merle the adult; his talk was fun, light, silly, and hers was too at times, but scattered in her foolishness would be unexpected words of deep maturity, as if she was old beyond her years.

Out of sight behind the gallery door, Bridget pictured them. The old thin man, and the paint-spotted, wrinkled skin on the back of his hands, clutching the leather of his big armchair. At his feet, little Merle, gazing up at him, as if gazing at the moon, her skin smooth and fair. Merle was holding a thin, worn, but well-loved paint brush, Eric was explaining about oil paints, how each colour has a different nature, and must be treated with respect, as if they were all caged animals. About how paintbrushes can tame the beasts, and put them on the canvas, to make beauty, or power.

One thing that Bridget heard confused her utterly. She'd asked Merle about it later, as they walked home.

I might be lots of people, she'd heard Merle say to Eric, seriously. *Why do I have to be just one? I am lots of people and I love all of them and they love me.*

Bridget didn't hear Eric's reply, and when she'd asked her daughter about it, Merle shook her head, puzzled.

'Sorry, Mummy,' she said. 'I don't think I remember that. That's *funny*.'

And she'd wrinkled her nose, and giggled.

Another day, Bridget was surprised when she came out of the kitchen into the painting room, and found the old man laughing himself silly at something Merle had said.

He seemed to be better, and after a few days, the point was proven.

Bridget and Merle were at home, having supper.

They were talking about Eric when there was a knock on the door. The front door.

'That's odd,' said Bridget, getting up, because nobody ever used their front door.

She came back into the kitchen a few moments later, bringing Eric with her.

'Look,' said Bridget, 'speak of the Devil!'

'Mummy, that's rude!' cried Merle.

'No, it's just what you say when, well, when that happens.'

They fussed over Eric, and sat him down, and though he refused food, he accepted a cup of tea with a smile.

'Well, look at you!' Bridget said, after a while. 'All dressed up!'

'Mummy, *that's* rude,' said Merle, but the old man laughed.

'I thought I should make an effort,' he said.

Eric wore a smart black suit, obviously quite old, but still presentable, and a clean white shirt. His shoes were clean, and almost shiny.

'So, to what do we owe the pleasure?' asked Bridget.

'Does there have to be a reason for a friend to call on another friend?'

Merle tugged her mother's sleeve.

'Mummy, *is* Eric our friend?' she whispered.

Bridget laughed.

'Of course Eric is our friend.'

'But actually, there are two reasons for me being here.'

He cleared his throat and had another sip of tea.

'For the first, I have come to thank you, for helping me.'

'But of course we were going to help you,' Bridget said. 'You don't need to thank us.'

'But I do. Not just for the food, and so on . . . Maybe I should explain. I have not painted anything for years . . .'

He hesitated, waiting for some kind of response.

'But that painting . . .?'

'I have been working on that painting for a long time. About a year. But let me put that in perspective for you. Before I began this painting, I had not painted anything, *anything*, in over twenty-five years.'

He was silent for a time, perhaps, thought Bridget, remembering things that he would rather not remember.

'When I was young,' Eric said sadly, 'the pictures poured out of me. Like water. I could not stop them. I could not paint fast enough to paint everything that was in my head. I felt like a magician, making magic. From nowhere, images would come, and in a few hours or days, another object existed in the world where none had existed before. Like magic.

'I painted portraits, landscapes, still life, I painted everything. Then, I made a little money with some simple pictures. For someone like me, it was unbelievable. I was born in a poor house, you see. I begged on the streets until I realised that I could earn more by sketching. Suddenly, I had everything.

'I was married then. My wife was young and beautiful, and we had three beautiful girls, almost as beautiful as Merle here.'

Merle giggled at this, and sat up straighter.

'I had everything, and for a time, for a very fair amount of time, we were happy. Then . . .'

He paused.

Bridget looked at Merle, briefly, then back at Eric.

'Then what?' she asked.

'My wife died. With the birth of our fourth child. She was perhaps too old, and . . . well. And I stopped painting. But you know, it wasn't just losing Martha that stopped me painting. Something else died then, with her. The ideas stopped coming, I was confused, I didn't know what to paint, but it was worse than that.

'One day, after a year or two had gone by, I realised I no longer wanted to paint. At all. I had had enough. The well, if you understand, had run dry. That was the worst thing. I no longer wanted to be that magician.'

Bridget nodded, but frowned.

'But this painting . . .?'

Eric shrugged.

'Maybe the well filled up again.' He winked. 'Maybe. Because about a year ago, I picked up a pencil, and I made a sketch. In about half an hour I sketched out that whole painting. The next day, I built the wooden structure on which it sits. The day after, I began to paint. It has taken me a year to finish it.'

'Finish it? Finish it?' cried Merle. 'Have you finished it?'

Eric nodded, smiling.

Then he laughed spontaneously.

They laughed too. Merle clapped her hands.

'Which brings me to my second reason for coming here

today. I have been approached by the National Museum. They are very interested in my new painting. Without being modest, they are of course interested to see what the great Eric Carlsson has been up to in twenty-five years. There is talk that it will hang on the grand staircase in the museum, adorning that splendid marble space. It will be the very first and last thing that visitors to the museum will see.'

'But what does this have to do with us?' Bridget asked.

'Because tomorrow I have some gentlemen from the museum coming to view the painting. And I should be honoured if you, both of you, would be there, as my neighbours. As my friends.'

Merle almost exploded.

'Oh, can we, Mummy? Please say yes!'

Bridget laughed, and held her daughter's hand.

'We'd be honoured. But tell us, what is the painting called? Does it have a title?'

'Yes,' said Eric. 'It is called *Midwinterblood*.'

Eleven

In the dimly lit room where Eric Carlsson's painting towered above the figures viewing it, there was silence.

The three men from the National Museum stood on one side; Eric, Bridget and Merle stood on the other.

The eldest of the men from the museum cleared his throat.

'Can you explain a little about it, Mr Carlsson?'

Eric nodded, stepped forward slowly, supporting himself on a stick.

'It is a scene from legend, from the sagas. It depicts the sacrifice of King Eirikr, on this very island here, to appease the gods, and to appease the people, after his crops failed for the third year in a row.

'It is a blood sacrifice, because after two lesser sacrifices, after the previous famines, the high-priest has declared that nothing else will suffice. To appease the gods, you see.'

The man from the museum inclined his head.

'Sacrifice. That's a somewhat . . . out-dated . . . notion, isn't it? In this modern world?'

'Out-dated?' echoed Eric. Suddenly, he felt very old. He felt that he didn't understand.

'The theme is old, but not out-dated,' he explained, feeling bewildered. 'And it refers to the island, *this* island,

161

whose very name is written in blood!'

'Really?' said one of the men.

'Indeed. People think the name of this island means "blessed", and so it does, but "blessed" does not mean what people think it does. In the old tongue it was "bletsian" and before that "blotsian" and before that, just "blod". It means sacrifice. Sacrifice.

'To bless means to sacrifice, and in blood.'

There is a pause. A long pause.

Then, 'Good. Well, thank you for your time here today, Mr Carlsson.'

With that, they left.

Merle and Bridget went soon afterwards, leaving Eric alone. Bridget tried to explain to Merle that Eric was tired, and needed to rest.

Eric sat in the darkening room staring up at his masterpiece.

Sacrifice, he thought. Out-dated?

Young upstarts from the city. Just because we have entered the modern world, have we done with suffering? Have we done with love, and loss? Have we done with wars? Then, there will be sacrifice! And when a parent works themselves to death to feed their child? Sacrifice?

And when a mother *dies* in childbirth?

Sacrifice.

He shook his head.

'Well,' he said bitterly to the dusky room. 'So it is.'

Bridget and Merle saw nothing of Eric for several days.

Then, one morning, as they came downstairs for breakfast, they saw a letter on the doormat.

It was addressed to Eric Carlsson, and had been opened, but turning it over, they saw their own names on the back of the envelope, and a short note, in Eric's hand.

My friends. Here is their answer. The fools! Yours ever, E.

Bridget opened the letter, and read the official response from the men from the National Museum. She skimmed through the formalities, to the conclusion.

The whole thing is as unreal as an opera, one cannot believe what is happening, one cannot connect emotionally with what is taking place. Midwinterblood *is a creepy, scandalous scene of dubious historicity and is no more relevant to us, modern men, than a scene of cannibalism from the darkest Africa.*

  Tor Bearvald, National Museum

Merle hopped about at her mother's side.

'What is it, Mummy? What does it say?'

Bridget stroked her daughter's hair.

'I'm afraid it's some bad news for Eric.'

Twelve

After breakfast, during which Bridget said not a word, she told Merle to go up to her room, and to play with her hare, until she came home again.

Merle went upstairs, her eyes wide with wild imagination.

❧

Bridget walked up and down the hill, to the western side, and straight around to the side door of Eric's church.

She found him, still sitting in the chair, in front of the painting.

She put her hand to his cheek, gently, and then snatched it away. He was cold.

There was no sign of violence, or other harm, and she knew that he had died from grief.

In his hand, was a thin, worn, well-loved paintbrush.

❧

She gently reached back again, and closed his eyelids, shutting their final dead view of his masterpiece, the masterpiece for which he had given everything.

For which he had sacrificed himself.

Suddenly there were footsteps, and Merle ran into the room.

'You didn't make me promise,' she said.

'Oh, darling, come here,' Bridget said, and they rushed into each other's arms, the small girl understanding some of what was going on, and feeling the rest.

They stayed that way, for a long time, and then Bridget straightened.

'Well, we'll have to try and sort things out,' she said, but Merle wasn't listening.

Then Bridget looked at the paintbrush in Eric's hand, and now she saw what she had missed before.

The brush was still wet.

'Look, Mummy,' Merle said, pointing at the picture.

Bridget looked towards where Merle had spotted something.

Something had changed.

The vast splendid horror of the painting remains, but there, in the background, is a new figure. Standing on the gallery, just behind the king, leaning round a pillar, only half visible, is the face, the shoulder, and the arm of a small girl. She's holding an apple out towards the king, placing it on the balustrade of the gallery.

She looks towards the king, smiling.

Her face is unmistakable.

It is Merle.

PART FIVE

The Unquiet Grave

_____

October 1848 – The Hunter's Moon

ॐ

One

After supper, the twins went up to bed.

Their parents were surprised at how docile they had become. At home, in Leipzig, the children had been becoming more and more of a handful, either fighting each other, or working on some mischief together.

Herr Graf was unwell; he had barely been able to complete his third symphony in time for its first performance at the Gewandhaus, and it would not have done to keep the Gewandhausorchester waiting; he may have shot to stardom as a young composer, but he was fully aware how easily his success, his fame, and his money could be taken from him again.

His doctor advised a health cure, and recommended an almost unheard-of island called Blest, in the far north. His doctor had met an Englishman who had been entirely cured of his tuberculosis after a spell there.

Herr Graf had a desire to travel alone, but Frau Graf was a strong-willed woman, and insisted that she and their son and daughter would not be separated. Now, he was glad that she had, because something was working a miracle not only on his own fragile health, but on the good humour of his children too.

'Good night, Pappa,' they said in unison. 'Good night, Mamma.'

And then they trotted up to the bedroom that lay at the far end of the single corridor in the upper floor of the house they were renting.

Yes, the children were enjoying their holiday, especially as it had meant dispensing with their tutor, when they would usually have been at school.

This was true, but there was another reason. They really liked the lady who their parents had arranged to look after them, a calm and kind lady called Laura.

Every night after they had said their prayers she would sit on the end of the bed and tell them a story.

Both children, brother and sister, thought that she was very beautiful, and listened, mesmerised, as she told her stories. The stories Laura told them were not like the dull ones they heard from their tutor, with boring children doing boring things.

No, the stories she told them were exciting. Stories full of wild adventures, of trips to mysterious lands, of brave heroes and wicked villains, and they loved them.

That night, Laura stood by the window, combing her hair. She was looking out at the night sky. She seemed more thoughtful than usual.

'Have you noticed, children? The nights are getting longer now,' she said, turning towards them, smiling. 'It is a hunter's moon tonight. And with a moon like this, I think there is only one kind of story to tell. A ghost story!'

The children giggled with delight.

'Would you like that?'

The children nodded.

'Very well, a ghost story it is.'

She grinned.

'I shall leave the curtains open. Blow out your candle, and I will tell you the story by the light of the moon.'

The children giggled again, and blew out the light.

Laura sat down on the end of the bed, combing her hair with long, measured strokes.

Two

'This is a story from the island itself,' Laura said. 'It's hundreds of years old, no one knows exactly. But everything I tell you is just as it happened.'

It is an old story, one of love, of forbidden love! And tragedy.

Once, there were two lovers. They were young, and each was beautiful in their own way. Their names were Merle and Erik. Merle was a delight; like some fresh and fast creature from the fields. She was slender, and her light brown hair streamed down her back.

When Erik first saw her, he was mending his fishing nets, at the quayside. She had just arrived back from the mainland, with her father, after a trip to the big city. As she stepped onto the quayside from the boat, their eyes found each other.

Neither smiled, but when Merle tipped her head on one side, still looking at Erik, he knew immediately that he had fallen in love. Merle's father, who was ahead of her, arranging some matters with his boatman, turned and saw the look that passed between them.

Erik glanced away, down at his fishing nets, and Merle hurried after her father.

'What were you doing?' Merle's father said. He was the richest man for many miles around, and it would not do for his daughter to be seen even looking at a fisherman. He was a wealthy merchant from the city, but he owned a house on the island too. That day they brought new items from the city with which to decorate their island retreat.

'I meant nothing, Father,' said Merle, and her father grunted disapprovingly.

They went home, but as they went, Erik straightened from mending his nets and watched Merle go. He noticed how light she was, how she moved, and he knew that what he felt was real, and true.

And yet, he also knew that trouble would come, for a love like theirs, between two such people, would never be allowed.

§

Laura paused and looked at the children.

'There are parts of this story,' she said, her voice dropping to a whisper, 'that are a little bit scary. And there are parts of this story, of which your parents might disapprove.'

She paused again. The children watched her, eyes shining. They had never conceived of such a thing before.

'If I tell you this story,' Laura said, 'it might be best if we agreed that you will not tell your parents. Is that a good idea?'

Both children nodded furiously.

'Good,' said Laura. 'Then I'll continue.'

Three

_____

'What could Merle do?' Laura said.

'Her father, who knew just how beautiful his daughter was, and what trouble that might bring, had always kept her locked up like a prisoner when they were in the city, and the island was like another prison.'

She had no friends, and there was so little to do. The house they had was the grandest on the island, but Merle quickly grew bored of its rooms, and its views. She longed to go outside and when she could, she would take long walks around the island, up to its highest point, looking across the western side, or to the meadows, empty and cool now that autumn had arrived. She would walk through the grass, and the hem of her long skirts would become wet.

But her favourite thing was to walk by the sea; along the beaches, by the rock-pools, through the woods that clung to the eastern shore. And the quayside.

She loved to watch the boats come in and out, but there was one boat that she always longed to see, the one that belonged to Erik.

Now it happened, that on a certain black day, though

it was not yet raining on the island, Merle saw a violent storm raging far out to sea. She worried for the fishermen, and for Erik, and worried more when she could not see his boat among those that had already returned.

She spoke to herself.

'Erik?' she murmured, to the wind.

Then, as she stood on the quayside, she heard a voice behind her.

'Well, so it is,' said the voice. She turned to see Erik. He smiled, shyly. He did not know how to talk to this fine young lady, did not know what he should say, though he knew very well what he wanted to say.

Merle tilted her head.

'Say his name and his horns appear!' she said, laughing, relieved. 'But where is your boat?'

'We put in at the south,' Erik explained. 'It was becoming too dangerous to make it further.'

Erik looked at Merle's skirts.

'But you are wet already,' he said, a question on his face.

'I was walking in the meadow,' Merle said, 'but it's nothing. It will quickly dry by the fire when I come home.'

She stopped, looked at the stones of the quayside.

'I was worried about you.'

Erik shrugged his shoulders.

'It is what we do,' he said. 'But a storm is coming. You ought to go home before it swings this way.'

Erik hesitated, then plucked up his courage.

'I could see you safely home.'

'Thank you,' said Merle. 'But I know the way, well.'

175

'I know you do,' Erik said, and then there was a silence between them.

Merle shook her head.

'But you may not walk me home,' she said. 'Father . . .'

She stopped.

'Goodbye,' she said. 'I am glad you are safe.'

She turned, and she walked back through the meadows, getting the hem of her skirt wetter still.

She was about halfway across the meadow, when, feeling a pricking on her neck, she turned. There, a fair way behind her, walked Erik, following her like a spectre.

She turned and walked on, and then turned again.

There was no doubt, he was following her, but at a distance.

She pressed on, her feet starting to chill thoroughly from the damp.

It grew dark with nightfall and thunderclouds as she approached the house, fingers of mist stroking her hair as she came out of the meadow. She hurried up the path to the front door, and was about to enter, when a low voice in the shadows spoke to her.

It was Erik.

She gasped.

'What are you doing here?' she asked, but Erik didn't answer this.

'What did you mean? What you said at the quayside. "Say his name and his horns appear . . ."?'

Merle smiled.

'It's just what people say. When they have been speaking of someone, and then they are there.'

'But horns? Am I a beast? A goat, or a ram?'

Merle looked at Erik. She noticed that the bottoms of his rough trousers were wet from the meadow grass too.

'But you're wet,' she said. She took a step closer to him.

'What kind of beast am I?' Erik asked again.

Merle's smile had gone.

She stepped closer to Erik, and then he gently placed his hands on her hips, and they kissed, for a long, long time.

When they broke away, Erik looked deep into Merle's eyes once more.

'You still didn't answer my question,' he said. 'What kind of beast am I . . .?'

Merle laughed too. She touched his forearm, very briefly.

She whispered, a grin on her face, laughter in her eyes.

'One that will be the death of me.'

Four

L aura stood and stretched her legs, setting the silver comb down on the chest of drawers in the twins' room.

They whispered to each other that it didn't seem like a ghost story at all, it seemed like a love story. Neither of them liked love stories.

And yet the full hunter's moon shone in through the window, and there was something about Laura, in her black dress with its purple hem, that made the telling scary. And there was something about the words she used to tell the story that made them realise something bad was going to happen.

Laura sat down again, pulling aside the skirts of the black dress, and continued.

The love that Merle and Erik had for each other grew, and grew, until it consumed them both.

It was hard for them.

Erik was always busy, either fishing or spending hours mending his nets. It was not an easy way to make a living, and left little time for pleasure.

And Merle's father watched her like a hawk watches a mouse in the meadow. He had sensed a change in her, and had sensed that something was going on. He was suspicious, and it became harder and harder for her to escape for even five minutes.

But they say that love will find a way, and they are right. Love always finds a way.

And so they continued to meet, in secret, mostly late at night, when Merle's father believed she was safely shut away in bed, and when Erik should have been sleeping so he had the strength to sail his boat the following day.

Very often they would meet at the top of the meadow, and, so as to avoid meeting anyone in the lanes, they would walk through the grass in the darkness, feeling their feet and the hems of their clothes getting soaked through.

When their feet were numb, they knew it was time to go home again, and they would part for another night.

One night, as they parted, Erik whispered to Merle.

'Say that you will never leave me,' he said, holding her hands.

'I shall never leave you,' said Merle.

'Is it so easy to say?' Erik said, surprised.

'It is, since it is you I speak of,' Merle answered. 'I will never leave you. No matter what happens, or where you go, or what you do. I will never leave you.'

'But it might not be so easy,' Erik said. 'Our love is forbidden. It might become impossible for us to be together.'

Merle shook her head.

'I will find a way,' she said. 'I will always find a way.'

That night, Merle slept deeply, but her dreams were strange and troubled.

She slept late into the morning, and her father, growing worried about her, came into her room. She did not wake.

He stood, looking down at his only child, and then his eyes fell upon her clothes, hanging over the back of a chair. He saw something and raised an eyebrow.

The hems of her skirts were soaking wet, which was odd, because when she had said good night to him the night before, they had been dry.

Five

——

The next night, Merle went out, after dark, as usual.

She had said good night to her father, as usual.

She walked to the top of the meadow, as usual.

She could not see Erik, so she waited.

She waited, and when he still did not appear, she began to grow worried.

Thinking there might have been some misunderstanding, she set off through the meadows by herself, the hem of her dress getting wet once again. She walked the entire length of the meadow, and back, and still she had not found Erik.

Eventually, desperately worried, she decided there was nothing else she could do but to hurry home.

A lonely figure was she, in the cold moonlight, the wind blowing the leaves from the trees in the dark, her wet skirts stroking the night grass.

She stepped to the door of the house, and slipped in, in darkness, and had her foot on the first stair, when suddenly a voice called from the drawing room.

'Daughter.'

A light flickered, and there was her father, sitting in the armchair, by the dying fire.

'What are you doing, daughter?'

Merle came forward, forming some explanation in her head, but then her words fell away.

She saw that her father was holding a pistol. He was pointing it at a figure who sat in the other armchair by the fire.

It was Erik.

Merle gasped. Erik looked at her sadly.

'Tell me,' her father said coldly. 'Tell me it isn't true.'

Merle shook her head.

'I cannot!' she cried. 'I cannot do that! I love him! I want to be with him forever.'

Merle's father stood.

'On the contrary,' he said. 'You will never see him again. Isn't that right?'

This remark he aimed at Erik, who stood also, miserably, looking at the floor.

Merle cried.

'No! Erik! What does he mean? Say it isn't true!'

But Erik shook his head. Yes, it might be true that love will always find a way, but so can hate.

'Your father is right,' Erik said, 'I'm sorry, Merle.'

He headed for the door, and Merle ran to stop him, but her father stood between them, waving the pistol wildly.

'Father! No!' Merle cried, but her father roared back in her face.

'Go to your room!'

He turned to Erik.

'And you! Just go!'

Merle ran upstairs sobbing.

The door closed behind Erik.

Her father was right; that was the last she ever saw of him.

ʕ

The following day, early in the evening, word came to the village that there had been a death, a drowning.

Erik had sailed as normal, with the other fishermen.

A storm had blown up and they had run for cover at the southern end of Blest, but Erik's boat had not returned.

Another fisherman reported seeing him in trouble, some way behind the rest of the fleet, which he said was strange, because Erik was the best sailor of them all.

ʕ

Two days later, Erik's body washed up on the southern shore, nibbled by the fish that he once caught.

A day after that, his boat was found, or the remains of it, in the shallows.

There were signs that the bottom of the boat had been stoved in, from inside, which again everyone found odd, because it had been well enough the morning he set out to sea; everyone swore to that.

Six

The twins stared at each other and at Laura.

'Do you mean, Erik drowned himself?'

Laura nodded, slowly, and the twins' eyes widened.

§

Erik knew their love could never be, and more than that, Merle's father had threatened to put Erik's whole family out of business. He was so powerful, he could have done it, just like that.

Merle was inconsolable.

Erik was buried in the tiny graveyard at the north of the island, and Merle went to the funeral.

Now there was nothing Merle's father could do to stop her, nothing with which he could threaten her. He had done the worst thing ever, and so Merle went to the funeral, unashamed of her forbidden love.

The other mourners gossiped and whispered, and as the funeral finished and everyone left, one of them spat at the ground in front of Merle's feet.

That night, it was a bright full moon, a hunter's moon, and Merle sat on Erik's grave, sobbing.

'I said I would never leave you,' she said, 'and I won't. I won't break my promise.'

She made a vow to herself, to Erik, there and then.

'If I have to wait for a year and a day, if I have to move the mountains, if I have to cross the rivers of the underworld, I will find a way for us to be together again.'

$$\backsim$$

Every night, at dusk, Merle would wander from her house, like a ghost, a mere shadow of her former beauty, and drift to the graveyard.

Every night, she would sit at Erik's grave, waiting, waiting for him to return. Eventually, she would fall asleep, her tears lost among the steady autumn rains that pattered onto the freshly turned grave soil.

Every morning, she would stagger home to bed, a cold and fevered wretch.

Her father tried to stop her, but no matter what he did or said, Merle took no notice of him.

The days turned into weeks.

The weeks turned into months.

The months turned into a year.

And still Merle spent every night weeping at her lover's grave.

As the year had passed however, something had happened to Merle, to her mind. It had grown tired, and been stretched beyond endurance, so that it tore, and so it was, a year and a day after Erik had been laid in the earth, that she went mad.

That night, as she slept on the grave, now well covered with grass, the gravestone softening gently with the turn of the days, she woke.

The moon was bright, almost as bright as day.

It was a clear, calm night, as still, indeed, as the grave, and she looked up to see a hare sitting on the grass, an arm's length away.

She knew immediately who it was, or rather, who she thought it was. In her delusion, she thought the creature was her lover.

'Erik!' she cried, and when the hare did not run away in fright, the belief that she was right grew in her. 'Erik!' she declared again, laughing, the tears streaming down her face.

She put out her hand, and the hare hopped closer, and sniffed her fingers. She leaned closer, and the hare came right up to her face, to her lips. They kissed, lightly.

'Erik!' she said. 'How clever!'

Then suddenly she realised something, and she sat up quickly. Now the hare bolted into the trees.

'But how,' she cried. 'How can I follow you? I must be with you, my love! How can I be with you?'

Though even as she said the words, she knew what she had to do. The idea formed in her head, like an apple ripening, and she knew what she had to do, and who she needed to help her.

On the hill, on the road out to the western isle, was an old woman, who knew the old ways.

They said she was a witch, and they were right.

Seven

The witch's house was the last on the right, going up the hill.

Merle sat by her fire, almost all the light gone from her eyes, her face pale and hollow, unrecognisable from the girl Erik had once loved.

The witch fussed around her, listening to her story, listening to what Merle asked of her.

There was silence for a very long time, and finally Merle lifted her eyes to the witch's.

'Well,' she said, 'can you do it?'

The witch seemed to think for a very long time, and then nodded. Slowly. Once.

'Yes, I can. Come back here, in a week.'

'So long?' asked Merle.

'The magic will take time to make.'

So Merle waited, another agonising week.

Every night, she sat on Erik's grave, waiting for him to come back as the hare again, but she only saw him twice, in the distant dark trees.

'Wait! Wait, my love!' she called. 'I will be able to follow you soon!'

And at the end of the week, she went back to the witch's house, and sat again in the chair by the fire.

'Well?'

The witch nodded, and from a cupboard she produced a glass jar of some cloudy liquid, purplish-black.

She nodded again.

'This will do what you require,' she said. 'Wait until nightfall. Go into the woods, or some other place where you will not be seen. Take off all your clothes, for you do not want to be caught in them when you wake again. Drink it. Drink it all. You will sleep.

'When you wake again, you will have assumed the form you desire, but you must make sure you hold that form in your mind as you go to sleep.

'Is that understood?'

Merle said nothing, and nodded.

Rising from her chair, she looked at the October sun, already sinking fast towards the western horizon.

She walked to the graveyard, sat on the grave, and waited for nightfall.

As she waited, she sang a song.

———

The wind doth blow today, my love,
And a few small drops of rain;
I never had but one true-love,
In a cold grave he was lain.

I'll do as much for my true-love
As any young girl may;
I'll sit and mourn all at his grave
For a twelvemonth and a day.
The twelvemonth and a day being up,
The dead began to speak:
'Oh who sits weeping on my grave,
And will not let me sleep?'
Tis I, my love, sits on your grave,
And will not let you sleep;
I crave one kiss of your cold clay lips,
And that is all I seek.

———

At darkfall, Merle stood, and delicately let all her clothes slip from her body, now thinner than ever, yet still something fresh and fleet, of the fields.

She lifted the jar to her lips, and without a further thought, she drank.

The jar fell from her lips, and she fell to the earth, clutching her throat and her belly.

The witch had not said it would be like this. With such pain, and yet she remembered the witch's other words, and so, even as she writhed in agony on the grave, thrashing around on the grass, she kept her desire in mind.

Her desired form.

A hare.

Eight

Next morning, Merle's father discovered that she was missing, and had not returned as usual from the graveyard in the early morning.

He organised a search for her, but though they searched the whole island over, and over again, all they found was her clothes, lying in a crumpled heap on the grave of the fisherman.

Her father collapsed on the grave, weeping.

From a short distance away, a hare watched the man crying.

After a while, the hare saw some other people pick the man up from the grave, and they all walked away.

The hare was alone. It hopped into the graveyard, across to one particular grave, the one where the man had been.

The hare seemed bothered, disturbed. It hopped around the grave, as if agitated, looking this way and that, looking, searching, searching for something, something that should have been there, and was not.

Finally, the hare sat on the grave, and waited.

And as it waited, a voice sang to it, from beneath the soil.
This was what it sang.

———

You crave one kiss of my cold clay lips;
      But my breath smells earthy strong;
      If you have one kiss of my cold clay lips,
      Your time will not be long.
Tis down in yonder meadow green,
      Love, where we used to walk,
      The finest flower that e'er was seen
      Is withered to a stalk.
The stalk is withered dry, my love,
      So, will our hearts decay;
      So make yourself content, my love,
      Till Death calls you away.

———

The story ends now, in tragedy.

For watching the hare, on the grave, was another pair
of eyes, and they belonged to the huntsman, out that night
with his gun, seeing what game was to be had.

As the hare slept on the grave, he took aim, and fired.
He smiled, because he knew his wife would be pleased
with him, with a hare to stew. He slung its body into his
sack, and walked home through the dark, whistling an old
folk melody.

With a last few whispered words, Laura finished her story, then she was silent.

The children stared at her, even wider-eyed than they had been before. Brother looked at sister, and sister looked at brother, then they both looked back at Laura.

Even in the dimness of the moonlit room, they could see she was crying.

Sister looked at brother, and brother looked at sister, and the twins decided without exchanging a word that they needed help.

They climbed out of bed, and tiptoed downstairs to find their parents.

'Did you notice?' they asked each other as they trod softly on the dark boards of the staircase. 'Did you notice her dress?'

They found their parents sitting in the drawing room, with another lady, one whom they hadn't met.

'Mamma. Pappa,' they said, together. 'Laura's crying. We think you should come up and speak to her.'

Herr and Frau Graf looked puzzled. Embarrassed.

'Who, dears, did you say is crying?' Frau Graf asked.

'Laura. The lady you have to look after us at bedtime. She was telling us a ghost story, and it wasn't even a proper ghost story. And now she's crying.'

Herr Graf stood.

'This is some kind of silly joke,' he said. 'One of your games. I want you to apologise right now and go back to bed.'

Then the twins began to cry.

'But it's true!'

'Children,' said their mother, more gently. 'This is Laura, here. She wasn't able to join us until today. I told you all this, don't you remember? Her mother has been sick, and she has only just arrived now.'

The twins turned to each other, then back to their parents. They looked at Laura suspiciously.

'Then who is it in our room?'

Now, their parents' eyes widened, and Herr Graf suddenly stormed upstairs. He was gone a little while, and then returned.

'Nothing,' he said. 'No one. As I said, one of your games.'

The children were too bewildered to answer.

'And did one of you spill your water? The boards are damp, at the foot of the bed.'

Nine

The twins would not apologise.

'This is not Laura,' they cried. 'Laura is upstairs! She looks nothing like her.'

'Stop it!' cried Herr Graf. 'Stop it! I want you to stop all this nonsense right now. What will Miss Laura think of you?'

But Laura sat quite unmoved on the sofa, a strange look on her face. She remained quiet.

'But what about the story she told us?' the twins suddenly realised. 'If we made all this up, then how could we know the story about Merle, and Erik? And about how they fell in love, but they weren't allowed to? And how Erik drowned and Merle went mad and then turned herself into a hare? How could we know that?'

Now their father was really angry.

'You have made it all up. You could make up any story and tell us a stranger told it to you! How dare you! How dare you embarrass your mother and me like this?'

'Children,' said Frau Graf, with one eye on their guest. 'I think perhaps you should go to bed now, and we can talk about it in the morning. When you're less tired. When we're all less tired.'

The children were about to protest, when the lady who

was really called Laura spoke.

'But, you know, Herr Graf, Frau Graf. There is such a story, though I haven't heard it in a long time . . .'

She stopped, looking puzzled.

'Only it was . . . rather different . . . from the one your children have just told us. It all happened just so, except that the reason their love was forbidden was not because Erik was poor. Merle was rich, but so was Erik. He wasn't a fisherman, and . . . well, he wasn't Erik. He was she. Erika.

'She was a nobleman's daughter. Their love was forbidden, because, well . . .'

She broke off, looking at the children. It was not the sort of thing they should hear. Laura remembered the story a little better now.

'She was beautiful too, they say. And always dressed so well, though she always wore the same dress, a favourite one.'

The children were silent.

Outside, a lady in a black and purple dress listened to the silence of the house.

From somewhere, a long way away, came the scream of a wounded hare.

It sounded so human.

The lady shook her head, thinking of her lover who had lost her mind, and become a lithe creature of the shadows.

'Well,' she said, sadly. 'So it is.'

PART SIX

The Vampire

10th Century – The Snow Moon

One

I am old now.

I am old now, and the things which happened under the weak light of the snow moon when I was a little girl have drifted far downstream. And yet, when I close my eyes, I see it all before me, once more.

Maybe there are things I have forgotten.

Maybe there are some things, things which have passed from my memory, and now exist nowhere. I am the oldest of the clan, and when I die, my memories will die with me, unless I have passed them on to the memory of others, through story.

So I have. I have told many stories in my life, and those stories that I have told, well, they will live on in the younger ones.

But there are some stories I have never told.

There is one story, one story . . .

There is one story which some people know a little of, but of which only I know the whole truth, and I will take that truth with me to whatever it is that lies in wait for us, when we close our eyes for the last time.

Two

———

Either the snows were early and heavy that year, or the boats were late returning, because the long meadows were almost impassable.

But no. It was the snow moon, I remember that, so it was the boats that were late. That was why it took the whole village to pull the longships up onto the cold meadows, grey in the half-light.

Even Eirik and I helped, though we were less than ten winters, I'm sure.

We had been sitting on the Outlook, waiting and wanting to be the first to see the ships return after the viking was over for the year.

They were so late. So late!

And with every day that they did not return, the village became a more and more silent place.

It was simply not possible that every ship had been lost. That none would return. Of course, from time to time, an expedition lost one, or even more, boats; it was dangerous to go viking. But to lose the whole fleet of ships? Impossible!

And yet, as the days turned over, and the nights grew so long that they almost touched each other, unspoken thoughts became muttered words, which became cries of woe!

They have abandoned us!

They have been lost to the middle-earthers!

They have been swallowed by the Krake!

But Eirik and I did not believe these cries. The ships had returned every autumn, and they would return this one too, even if autumn had become winter.

Finally, as we sat on the Outlook, watching the sun barely skimming the sea, Eirik saw the masts.

He tugged my sleeve and we stood, breathlessly, and counted.

We waited until they were closer, and then, still not saying a word, we counted again.

They were all there.

'Go!' I screamed, and I ran with my brother down the hill, and burst into the longhouse at the crossways.

'Mother!' we cried together, as we so often did, 'Mother! They are come back!'

Our mother turned from her work at the fireside, among the other women, and stood, one hand holding a knife, the other the limp body of a hare, half skinned.

It took time for the words to mean anything to her.

I can see her lips now, in the eye of my mind, as I picture how she repeated the words we spoke, but without sound.

'They are come back.'

'Mother! Come on!'

By now others in the northern harbour had seen the masts too, drawing in fast on a westerly wind. Shouts came from the lane.

Mother yelped then, as if she'd burned her hand. She

dropped everything, and we all ran into the snow, joining the shouts and the cries of the whole village, the young, the old and the women, as their men returned.

Then, there they were!

Father, standing on the prow of his ship, waving to us, to his village, as a chieftain should.

'Eirik!' his cry came across the wind, 'Eirik! Melle! We are home!'

He was laughing.

We tried to call back, but the wind was against us, and he shook his head.

The keel scrunched on the stones, the hull breaking the ice-plates, the round beginnings of a frozen sea, swarming in the shallows.

Father leapt.

He leapt from the great height of the prow, down to the stones, and strode towards us.

'Bring the wheeled sleds!' he roared, but we had run to him, and threw our arms around him.

'My boy! My girl! How much have you grown!'

He laughed again, and we stared up into his eyes.

Eirik laughed back, I think.

I just smiled.

I know that's how it was with Eirik and me.

Eirik's tools were his hands, his legs, his arms.

My tool has always and always only been one thing, my thought.

And with that thought, I could see that although Father was laughing, something was bad inside, something that he did not want to be. And yet was.

Three

The viking had been a good one.

All twelve ships had returned, laden with wonders, and the losses had been but six men, two of them from sickness.

And there was someone else, someone new.

As Father and Eirik and I walked up the beach, and Father greeted the village elders, there was a crunch of steps behind us, and a man that Eirik and I had never seen strode past us.

He looked down at us, and I was afraid immediately, I do not know why. I think, and I have thought about this for years, that it was the way that he looked at us.

He looked at us as though he wanted us. The way a wolf wants meat.

It frightened me, but I think it excited Eirik.

'Father!' he whispered, 'Who is that? Where did you find him?'

'His name is Tor,' our father said. 'And I want you to have nothing to do with him. You hear?'

We nodded, and stared secretly at the figure. He was tall and strong, maybe even taller and stronger than Father. He looked much older than Father too. He was dark haired, and his skin darker than ours, as if he had seen much sunshine, for a long time.

Eirik and I believed him to be a stranger.

That was our guess, that he was someone that Father had shown pity for on his travels, and had brought back, and yet we were wrong, because the elders recognised him, and some even put their arms around him.

And he knew their names. So we knew he had been to Bloed Isle before.

'Bring the sleds!' roared Father again. 'We have little light.'

He was right.

The short weak day was nearly done, and there were twelve ships to unload and beach.

Before long, we worked by torchlight.

The whole village toiled.

Small boats put out to and from the ships, ferrying the spoils back to land.

Meanwhile, the shipmen set the wheeled sleds into the water at the prow of Father's boat, and then the ropes were tied fast.

Taking a cue from the waves, the hardest part was swiftly done, lifting the ship's prow onto the sled.

Then the hauling began, with great shouts and songs to make it easier, and everyone, *every one* of the village had some place on some rope, all but the smallest barn, and even those tiny children held the torches by which we worked.

I remember it.

What a night! The great ships towering above my head. The orange torchlight on the snow, black smoke coiling out of sight into the shadow-blue sky, the smell of the men, the smell of the salt water on the ships, the barnacles on their hulls like the stars in the heavens, our hands freezing to the ropes.

The songs, the laughter, the curses.

But I remember one thing above all others.

We worked next to our father, the Chieftain, so proud and happy to see him again after so many months.

We were struggling just then. It was the last ship, the last to be pulled from the water, and dragged through the piling snow, like a huge dead wooden whale.

Maybe the men were tired, but we struggled.

Suddenly the stranger, Tor, was there.

'Not enough strength, Wulf?' he said to Father.

Father ignored him.

'Have your men lost their power?'

'Get on a rope, Tor,' Father said, but Tor didn't.

He rubbed Eirik's hair with one of his massive hands.

'Nice boy,' Tor said.

Eirik smiled, and father threw down his rope, and in a moment, he stood with his face a hand's breadth from Tor's.

Everything went quiet, and there was a long silence.

The creak of the ropes, the shouts and songs, even the rush of torch fat seemed to go quiet.

Then Father spoke.

'Get on a rope, Tor,' he said.

Tor looked deep into Father's eyes, and then, not looking away, bent down and picked up the rope.

There was a shout, we heaved, and the boat slipped into

its safe haven in the snows of the meadows.

The work was done, and I remember just one more thing about that evening.

How, as Tor walked off towards the longhouse, Father watched him go.

Then he spat on the ground where Tor had stood.

Four

The feast flew. Soared into the night like a ravening bird, like a fire flame, like the spread of a plague, a party as wild as the night outside was long.

It seemed to go on for days.

It felt like the longhouse had never been empty, not all those many months when the men were away on the knarrs.

Suddenly, in an evening, it was a place of firelight and joy and warmth; a small ship of life, making ready to sail through the dark and snow of winter, winter that was prowling outside, just on the other side of the smoky thatch.

Not one, but two pigs were slaughtered, and the smell of their roasting filled the highest corner of the longhouse.

Flower beer flowed like the streams from the hill, the bread was warm, and there were even apples from the western isle, stored in barrels against the winter.

Father sat at the middle of the long table, with Mother at his elbow.

We sat with the other children, to the side, but we did not mind.

Father was home! And we could see everyone and everything.

I looked at him again, closely. There was something in his eyes, I knew, something in his heart.

'Eirik,' I whispered. 'What is wrong with Father?'

But Eirik! Oh, he knew nothing.

Eirik was always for doing, not for thinking.

Faced with a runaway dog, Eirik would spend ages happily chasing it round the meadows, whereas I . . . I would have found a bone and let the dog come to me.

That was Eirik and me.

So he saw nothing.

'What?' he said. 'Wrong? Nothing is wrong. Look!'

And maybe he was right. The hall was the happiest I had ever seen it, and it glowed with all the good colours; browns and reds and earths and yellows.

Father stood up, a skull of pig blood in his hand.

He turned to the room.

'Our strength was great!' he cried. 'And we are with you again! Yet we lost six men, and this feast we honour to those six. Hakon! Kar! Magnus! Sigurd! Björn! Gilli!'

With each name, there was a roar, and cups were clattered and skulls were scattered, and father drank the name of each of his fallen men, in blood.

Yet, there was still no mention of the newcomer, this Tor. And even I, as a child, knew this was wrong.

Father waved a hand for silence.

'Where,' he said, and I can see him doing it now, his voice dropping to a whisper, 'is Leif Longfoot?'

Then, pointing across the room, he cried.

'Leif! Our skald! We must have words! Give us words to remember our long voyage, and our great deeds, and to remember those who we lost.'

There was Leif, walking into the centre of the longhouse, to stand by the firelight, to give us his words.

He was a beautiful man, tall and thin, not one for fighting, though he fought with the others when it was needed so. But his tools were words; those mysterious gifts from the gods, and while most men merely learned how to use them, Leif was one of the wizards who had learned the secret of how to make magic with them.

He stood by the fire, and waited for silence.

Then, he cried.

'Hwaet!'

And so, we all knew his words were about to begin, and wonderful they were to hear.

> *On a good day*
> *is born that great-souled lord*
> *who hath a heart like his;*
> *aye will his times*
> *be told of on earth,*
> *and men will speak of his might.*
>
> *Unfettered will fare*
> *the Fenriswolf,*
> *and fall on the fields of men,*
> *ere that there cometh*
> *a kingly lord*
> *as good, to stand in his stead.*

Cattle die
and kinsmen die,
land and lieges are whelmed;
when Wulf
to the wide waters went,
many a host was harried.

His poem told us all of the fears and fates that had beset Father and his men since we had last seen them, at the rushing start of the summer.

As we listened, I fingered the necklace at my throat, that one that Eirik had made for me from bone, a leaping hare.

I saw Tor rise from his place.

I also saw that Father had seen, and was carefully watching him as he stalked around the longhouse, behind the tables. He had been sitting opposite us, and somehow I knew where he was heading.

By the time he stood behind Eirik and me, rubbing his hands through our hair, the whole room was silent.

Leif's last words died and floated away like just another spark from the fire, and then there was a terrible time of nothing.

Father did not rise, but spoke from where he sat.

'Tor. What do you mean by this?'

We could feel his hands in our hair, and I felt for Eirik's hand, and he felt for mine, as we did not understand what was happening.

Then Tor's voice rang out, flew above our heads, back towards Father, towards the whole longhouse.

'These children,' he said, 'are mine.'

Five

———

The feast foundered.

I saw many things.

Mother, looking away, looking away from Tor, looking away from us, from Father.

I saw how Father leapt across the table, scattering everything, the food, the drink, the knives, and then how he was in front of us, leaning across the table to Tor.

I hadn't seen him pick up a knife, but there was a knife in his hand all the same, and its point was at Tor's throat.

Despite which, it was Tor who spoke first.

'Do you deny it?' he whispered, his voice as thin as a reed by the water.

I was so close, I could see the point of the knife wavering, wavering, as Father breathed heavily.

Then, with a roar, he threw the knife into the dirt at his feet, and shoved Tor backwards, away from us, sending him into the wall.

He staggered, feeling his throat, as if the knife were still there.

Father turned to the hall.

'Our guest forgets himself. Yet we can forgive this.'

There was something wrong about the way he spoke the word guest.

'Yes. We forgive. But . . .'

He turned to Tor.

'For this night only. For this night, this night is a time of remembering and goodness, and we will not spoil it with stains of the tongue.'

He turned to Leif.

'Thank you, Leif. How the gods use your voice I shall never understand. Give us music now. Give us songs!'

Others came forward then, and with the flute, the pipes and the drum, music was made.

I looked behind us.

'He's gone, Melle,' Eirik whispered to me, just as I saw the truth of that. It was so, Tor had left the hall, in disgrace.

'But what did he mean?' I whispered to Eirik. 'What did he mean?'

Eirik's eyes were wide. I knew he knew no more than I.

Just then, the old woman whose name was Sigrid leaned over to us.

'Do you not know? Has your father not told you?'

Her face was lined, having seen the weather for so long a time, and yet, her eyes told us of horror, or of shock.

'Has your mother not told you?'

We shook our heads, together, as we often did.

'No,' we said.

Sigrid's eyes narrowed.

'But you must know. Tor is your father's brother. He is your uncle.'

The songs continued late into the night, but I heard not a note, nor whispered a word more.

All I knew was the warmth of Eirik's hand in mine, and we both shook from the not knowing.

Six

———

The tale was not one we could get from our father, nor from our mother, but as the days of the snow moon turned, we stole the story, like the hooded crow does in the midden, in scraps.

Tor, our father's brother, had left the village, had left Bloed when Eirik and I were barely born.

Something had happened, and here even though we pestered Sigrid and others besides, we could not learn the whole of the happening.

Yet we knew enough.

Our father had become chief, and had taken our mother as his, though Tor had wanted her for himself.

Yet, being the older brother, and having the right to choose, he took our mother.

There had been no children. That was what we kept hearing.

There had been no children.

And every night, Wulf, our father, would drink more and more flower beer, brewed from the dragon plant on the western isle, and had grown into himself.

During this time, we heard, our mother was looked after by Tor, who offered her comfort where there was none, and love, where it had died.

214

And then, at last, a miracle occurred, and our mother became heavy.

Nine months later, and the miracle was made two-fold, as not one of us, but two of us slipped out of Mother's belly and onto the rug by the fireside.

They said we held hands as we emerged into the world.

They said that Father cried.

They said that Mother wept.

They said that the priest swore, because he had only prepared a single totem. Only expecting one child, he had not made magic for more.

As I was the first out into the world, he wrapped me in the skin of a hare, and pushed a hare's skull into my hand, and a hare's small leg bone into my mouth.

'What of the boy?' Mother had asked.

The priest had shaken his head.

'The gods did not see another,' he said.

'But he will be king one day!' Father cried.

'That may be,' the priest said. 'But he will be so without a totem.'

'That cannot be!' Father shouted. 'I have my raven! My father had his fox! Everyone must have a totem. Most of all a king!'

And then, we are told, that the priest thought for a long time. He nodded to himself.

He looked at the pair of us, wriggling on the wet rug, and spoke.

'Then you must give him a strong name, instead. Give him a name from the old stories. From the sagas. A name of strength. A name of eternity. A name with powerful meaning. You should call him Eirik: Forever Strong, The One King, and that will be enough to protect him. Not only in this life, but in other lives yet to come.'

It was only later, a little later, that the bad time began.

Tor declared that Eirik and I were his children. He claimed that he, not Wulf, had fathered them on our mother.

He demanded satisfaction, he demanded that we be given to him, and he did not care who he abused or whose honour he insulted to get his way.

Eventually, he was banished from the island, for a time of no less than three years.

He was taken out with the viking, as it left one leaf moon, taken to be abandoned at the farthest reach of the voyage.

He was never seen again.

Seven years passed and he was never seen again.

And then, this viking, there he was, found in the sunny lands of the middle earth, his skin tanned, his beard shorn, and he demanded his return to Bloed.

They refused at first, but honour bound them to obey, and so they brought our uncle home. Our uncle? Our father?

Seven

The turning of the days became heavy and thick.

The short tide of daylight was grey and grim, as an unborn violence took root in the soil beneath the snows.

It was unseen, but it was felt by all, and it grew.

Very soon, it would burst up out of the ground.

Eirik and I clung to each other.

'What will be?' I whispered to him one night, as we lay in our bed, in the small room behind the longhouse. Our parents slept soundly, beyond the fire, but Eirik and I were full of fear and of wondering.

'Why do they not speak to each other?' Eirik whispered back.

It was true. Mother and Father were not speaking.

Tor strode round the village as if he were the chieftain, not Father. Some sneered at him as he passed, others took his hand in friendship, and so the village grew divided, and quiet, and brooded.

Eirik and I shivered and shook, and waited for something to happen, and we did not have long to wait.

One night, the violence that had been growing between Father and Tor erupted.

At meal time, as we sat and silently chewed our food, the doors opened and there stood Tor.

I heard my father say, 'Name him, and he's always near.'

Heads hung, others lifted.

Words were muttered, as once more, Tor walked around the tables, and out into the centre, by the fire.

He stood facing Father and then, without looking at us, his hand pointed in our direction.

'Those barn,' he said, 'are mine. They are my seed, and mine to own. I will have them to me.'

Father stood.

Now all eyes were lifted, and all hands shook.

My father stood and walked around the high table, into the centre of the great longhouse, and walked up to Tor, till their toes touched.

He said a single word to Tor, but no one knew what that word was, so quietly did he speak.

And then they were on each other.

I could not see who struck first, so fast it was, and it mattered not, because in a moment they were one beast, rolling in the dirt.

It would have been usual at such a fight for shouts to ring out, for voices to cry and for hands to hammer on the tabletops.

But not this time. This time there was silence, and the only sounds were the sobbing of our mother, and the grunts of the men grappling.

I felt for Eirik's hand and he felt for mine, just as our father's and our uncle's hands felt for each other's throats.

It didn't take long.

As they rolled, I wondered why it was that our father, some years older than his brother, seemed the younger. His skin was younger, his back was straighter, his arms stronger.

And his hands.

He was astride Tor now. Like a horse. Even at the awful moment, I remember that I thought it looked as if he rode a horse.

But he didn't, he rode a man, and as I fingered the hare at my throat, Father's fingers closed around the throat of his brother, and squeezed.

They squeezed until the blood went from his fingers, so it looked like hands of bone, hands of a skeleton that tightened, and dug into Tor's neck.

Tor's eyes opened wide, his mouth opened wide.

His legs scrambled at the mud, but his arms were pinned to his sides by Father's legs.

Tor's heels ripped the earth of the floor like the furrows of the farmer's field.

Then they stopped.

Nothing moved.

No one moved, or even breathed.

Then, slowly, finally, Father's weight shifted, and his hands let go of his brother's throat. He sat back, still astride the horse.

Tor's eyes stared at the ceiling, seeing nothing.

They could not see now, so they did not see the tears that ran down his brother's cheeks.

Eight

Then came the beginning of wonders on Bloed Isle!
We buried Tor in the long meadow, in a mound some way from the others, though with the proper rites, for his was royal blood after all.

There was a short silence then, a short silence of days, in which a fresh snow fell, quickly hiding the bare earth and stones of Tor's grave, and it felt as if we had been blessed.

Blessed, because we could breathe again, put the blood behind us, and breathe again, blessed.

But we were not blessed, and the blood was yet to come.

I do not remember what happened first.

Whether it was a dog or a cow.

No. I do remember now. Strange how walking the journey once more brings back both shade and detail.

One day, someone came to the great longhouse, holding the carcass of a dog.

'It went mad,' they said. 'It went mad and began to claw at the cattle. I had to break its back with a spade before it would stop.'

That was the first.

The day after, the cattle began to give a great lowing, a terrible moaning, an awful sound, as when they give birth, though the calf moon was still long away, across the other side of the darkness of winter.

The sound rose and fell, rose and fell all day, until we went into the meadows, and saw that the cows were all in the fold, the winterfold, nearest to which was Tor's grave.

My father spoke.

He raised a hand to a cowherd, a young boy.

'Manni,' he said, 'take them. Put them in another fold. That one, yonder. Do it now.'

Manni did as he was bid, and was almost trampled by the cows as they stamped their way from the one fold to the other. Once in the far fold they grew quieter, though still a great cry would come from them, a sound that haunted us, throughout the black night.

In the morning came the first of the blood.

Another dog was dead, but not, this time, at his master's hand.

It was one of the bitches. She was found by the midden, with her throat torn, and her blood taken.

Father ordered the carcass to be burned, not thrown in the midden.

Eirik and I looked at each other, our eyes gaping.

'Why is he doing that?' Eirik whispered to me.

I tilted my head to one side.

'I do not know, brother. But I am afraid.'

Eirik took my hand, and we walked on through the short day, but by nightfall, there were to be more strange wonders.

The dried fish in the buttery were found rotting, the butter was rancid.

But these were just portents, mere omens, and the worst was yet to come.

For it was that night, that someone said they had seen a figure stalking the long meadows. A tall, strong figure, with a dark face.

They said it was Tor.

That morning, as Eirik and I brushed bad dreams from our heads, we woke to the sound of screaming.

First, we ran outside, and saw the carcass of a cow, a whole cow, gutted and bled, lying in the lane right outside the longhouse. A trail of blood led towards it.

Voices cried and wailed, and muttered.

'Who has done such a thing?'

'Who could do such a thing? The beast is heavy! Who could lift it here?'

Then, another scream.

'Look! Oh! Look!'

Everyone gathered then at the side of the longhouse, upon which were written words.

They were shaky, tall and crazed, and they were written in the blood of the slaughtered cow.

'What does it say?' someone asked, someone without letters.

But no one dared speak it aloud.

It was too awful, and yet, Eirik and I knew the words, for we had letters.

I want my children.

That was all.

Nine

The days shortened and the nights lengthened, and tightened around us like a rope around a throat.

The wonders grew.

Any beast that went near Tor's grave went mad, and we were heavy to put it to death.

Sightings of the dark figure became common, though no one actually saw Tor face to face, to say it was him. But they said he moved like a shadow between the barns and the houses, there one moment, gone the next.

Two more beasts were found, ripped apart, their blood sucked away from them.

The first was another dog.

The second was a winter hare.

When I saw it, something entered my heart, a small splinter of ice, and no matter how hard Eirik held my hand, it would not go away.

I knew what it meant.

Two days later, as we were returning from the fishing boats in the early evening, a scream came to us from the longhouse.

We were twelve, and without fear: we ran into the great hall, almost bursting the doors from their hinges.

There stood Sigrid, the old, screaming and screaming.

When she saw us, she fell to the ground, silent.

We saw what she had been screaming at.

There was a body on the dirt. A human body this time, a young girl, called Bera. And over Bera's body crouched Tor.

As we burst in, he lifted his head, and we saw the blood running freely from his lips, from where he had been drinking from Bera's throat.

He stood, and pointed at us.

At Eirik, I mean. And me.

Then he spoke, in a voice thick, choked from the blood that was still trickling down inside.

'I want my children.'

He walked towards us.

Father, and some of the other men, were quick, and grabbed burning logs from the fire, waving them at Tor, thinking that fire would harm this evil, and they seemed to be right.

Tor squealed like a pig that has been cut, and suddenly was gone.

Just gone – we did not see how, as if he had moved so fast that our eyes could not see it.

'We all sleep in here tonight,' said Father. 'That way we will be safe.'

So we did as Father said, but he was wrong.

We were not safe, and when we woke, another youngling, a boy called Jon, was gone, right from where he slept among us.

Ten

—

In the morning, no one would look at us.

At Eirik, and me, I mean.

The wailing and the crying being too unbearable, we went outside, and found Father, Leif and some of the other men, the biggest and the strongest.

'We have a short time,' Father said. 'That's all. A short while of daylight, to put a stop to this.'

The men nodded.

'But how?' asked one. 'How do we kill that which is already dead?'

Father grunted.

'There are old ways,' he said. 'There are old ways, written in the sagas. Is that not so, Leif?'

Leif nodded.

'It is true. All we can do is to believe they will work for us, here, today.'

'So what do we do?'

'What do we do?' repeated Father. 'We pay Tor a visit. That's what.'

So we left for the long meadow, and Eirik and I were glad to go, for as we left, we heard the villagers muttering and pointing.

'It's them he wants. It won't stop till he has them.'

We came to the meadow.

The snow lay deep upon the ground, and everyone wondered at how Tor was able to come out at night, and not make a mark on the snow. Anywhere.

'He is a devil now,' Father said, shrugging. 'Who knows what things he can do? Enough! We dig!'

The men dug, first clearing the snow from the mound, then the sparse earth that had been scattered over the stones of the cairn, and then, making a chain of bodies, the large stones of the cairn were lifted away, one by one.

With all the cairn stones gone, it only was left to lift the stone lid.

'Wulf . . .?' began one man.

Others drew back. A waiting fear had crept into us all.

'What are we doing?'

'What if . . .?'

But Father stepped onto the lid. And stamped his foot.

'Whatever is in here. Whatever it is, it's not Tor. Not any more. And now, with daylight, it can do nothing. So stop belly-aching and help me lift this stone. For our children's sake!'

The lid was lifted, and there, inside the grave, lay Tor.

It was another wonder.

His body was uncorrupted. He looked as though he slept. That was all.

And yet, there was blood at the corners of his mouth.

Father turned to Leif.

'Did you bring them?' he asked, and Leif stepped

forward holding a leather bag.

Father took it from him, and pulled out a massive hammer, and two stout stakes, made of whitethorn, from the western isle.

No one helped my father.

He knelt down, to finish what he had begun.

He hammered the first stake right through Tor's chest, and deep, deep, deep into the soil beneath.

He took the second stake, and drove it hard into Tor's mouth, between his lips, which opened to take this offering. There was a crunch and a crack of bone, but Father did not stop hammering until only the very tip of the stake was pointing from Tor's mouth.

Father stood.

'Try walking now,' he muttered.

He turned to go.

'Come, children.'

And then to the others.

'Cover him up again. Just as he was. Then forget this place.'

Eleven

How those days were passed, I have no idea. Not even my journey of remembering can take me back to that darkest of nights.

There had been three days, that I do recall.

Three days, and nights, of no wonders, and it seemed that the old sagas were right. The way to stop the again-walker was to hold him to the ground, with stakes of magical thorn, if possible.

Very slowly, we began to recover, but then it all fell apart.

It had snowed, fresh snow, snow again and always.

And in the snow, one night, we found Matilda.

Her throat was gone, and most of her blood.

It was late as we went to bed, and Eirik and I went to sleep, as usual, holding each other's hands.

'When will it stop, Melle?' Eirik whispered to me through the darkness.

'Go to sleep, children,' said Mother, from across the room. Father stood, by the fire, sword in hand, his back towards us. He poked the fire with his sword, lost in thought.

'I don't know, Eirik,' I whispered back, right in his ear so only he could hear. 'But I'm afraid. Aren't you?'

But Eirik didn't answer.

Somewhere, out there, in the darkness, Tor prowled.

Looking for us.

For me, for Eirik.

It was always his way. His tools were his hands, and his arms and legs. My way was to think, his way was to do.

When I woke in the morning, and found that his hand was not in mine, I knew at once what he'd done.

I could see him waiting till even Father had gone to sleep, and I could see him getting up from our bed of furs and hay, and standing.

I think he probably didn't say anything before he went. His way was to do, not to speak.

But I think he probably paused to look down at me, one finger twined round my hare necklace, and then he stole out of the house, into the dark. He left me, alone.

He would have walked just for a little while, and then, finding Tor in the lanes, would have held his hand, turned, and set off, back towards the mound in the long meadow.

It might not have worked.

Tor might not have been satisfied, but it seemed that Eirik was right. Tor was content, in the end, to settle for just one of us, one of the children who might be his nephew, or might be his son.

For the wonders stopped, and the murders, and the hauntings.

᛫

I often think though, about that grave down in the long meadow.

Surely now, surely now that I am an old woman, and soon to stop telling stories and to go to the other side of sleep, surely those bodies have become bones?

I like to think of those bones.

The large ones, cradling the small ones, in their arms.

Father.

And son.

PART SEVEN

Midwinterblood

———

Time unknown – The Blood Moon

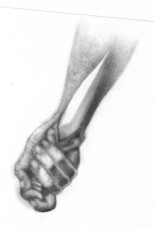

The Glorification of the Chosen One

T he drum beats.
      The horns call.
The moment has come.

The full blood moon hangs high in the always night sky, above the temple. It is a triple portent.

The full moon.

The winter solstice.

A lunar eclipse, casting the moon an ominous red.

Its light shines down on the writhing bodies below, a light strong enough to illuminate the scene, but without colour. Colour is brought by the torches that burn, on all sides, in the warriors' hands, on the walls of the temple.

The flickering light of the torches gleams on spear tips and sword hilts; there is the glint of metal, and gold. Gold is everywhere: the gilt of the two curled horns, whose sound appears to come from far away, though they are at the forefront of the crowd.

Their sound is blaring and constricted at once, a nasal high piping, which can only be designed to wake the spirits of the ancestors. These horns are played by the twins Ari and Arni, the torchlight picks out their blond beards as they tilt their chins to the heavens. They are dressed in long robes of midnight blue, blue caps pulled down tight on their heads, almost across their eyes, for they do not need to see. Not yet.

The high whine of their curled horns is underpinned by the low grunting of the three huge straight horns; bone covered in gold leaf, played by three men in long white robes, they arch their backs to burst each blast into the black sky.

The song of the horns, the three straight and the two curled, seems a cacophony at first, but slowly the complex repetition as the five horns step across each others' path in sequence begins to infect everyone's mind with a hypnosis, and this is good. For what is about to happen, they will need to be almost out of their minds.

Behind the musicians come seven dancing women, in the blue braided dress and red braided caps they wear when anyone is born, or wedded, or dies.

They link their fingers, intertwine them as they twist, already half-crazed by the music, half-crazed by their fear. Emotions streak across their faces; terror and ecstasy mingle on their lips, shine wildly in their eyes.

In front of the musicians, two small old men dance madly too. Dressed in skins, and fur boots, they are the shamans; their eyes stare blindly into the distance, for they don't see in this world, they see in other worlds.

There is more gold.

The warriors' shield bosses, with their shiny orbs; their ceremonial helmets gleam with the golden creatures that surmount each one: the boar, the fox, the raven, the eagle, the golden horns of a bull.

The warriors march slowly, seven on foot to match the dancers, the others come further behind, as if keeping their distance.

Gold too, on the walls of the temple; the decoration above the porch shows scenes from the old tales in elaborate designs of tangled foliage, and the rearing horses of the ancestors.

Gold are the monumental hounds, more like dragons than dogs, that sit on top of the pillars either side of the doorway.

Gold are the finials of the roof beams, the capitals of the columns, and gold are the things that hang in the single evergreen tree that grows outside the temple.

Look closer; these hanging things. They are three skulls, covered in gold leaf. One is that of a foal, two are those of men.

There is one more thing that burns bright with gold; the sled, upon which King Eirikr is dragged towards the stone table.

Four men, two in front and two behind, haul and heave at the sled, sliding it jerkily through the snow. They have only a few feet left to travel, and then Eirikr will have come.

Waiting for him are the two final figures in the ceremony.

Thorolf. The sage.

Dressed all in white, with mad white hair and long white beard, and his one white eye. His other, good eye glares down at the ground, waiting for the sled to appear before him.

Above his head, he holds the golden hammer of the gods.

At his neck, he wears the symbol of the sacred flower, for like Eirikr, he is a disciple of that cult, and worships, and consumes, the magical flower with its three fantastical petals, shaped like a dragon's head.

The symbol is a curling three-pointed device, one for each petal of the dragon flower.

The final figure.

The executioner.

Chosen by the selection of pebbles from a cooking pot, no one save the warriors knows who he is; he who drew the black stone from among the thirty white.

Robed entirely in red, with a red hood pulled over his head and across his face, he stands with head bowed low.

All he is, is a pillar of red cloth, red like the blood he will spill.

Wait! Look closer still. Something protrudes from the pillar; his forearm, and hand, and in his hand, his swordhand, he clutches a thin, sharp, curving blade, almost as long as to reach his elbow.

The sled is nearly at its place.

King Eirikr rises from the gilded throne upon which he has been riding.

He is covered in a massive fur of fox, and yet, as he stands, he slips the knot at its neck, and lets it fall to the wooden floor of the sled.

He is naked, yet he feels neither the cold of night, nor the deep of winter. His blood is pounding through his body. He tips his chin to the heavens, defiantly.

He is naked but for the narrow gold band gripping his head, the gold bracer of triple design, another symbol of the flower cult, the magic of which even now hurtles round his veins with the rest of his hot blood.

As if in an orgy of orchestrated genius, there is always a moment of silence before the violence and noise of the act itself.

Before battle, as the whole army takes in a breath.

Before the diver leaps into the water, and the sea pounds his eardrums.

Before the storm, the stillness in which a single bird calls.

Before the pains of birth, the brief rest between the spasms.

Before all the other instruments descend in a maelstrom, the faint and strangled chord from the bassoons.

Before the ice breaks, before the tree falls, before the sword lands.

It might only be a fraction of a moment, but that time can dilate, can swell and grow, can fill the world around it with its power, till it lasts for a lifetime.

And so it is with Eirikr.

He arrives.

The horns fall silent, the dancers cease, the warriors stop marching, and across that sudden enormous space float two whisperingly quiet discordant notes, from a pipe perhaps, from somewhere inside the temple.

Into that silence stumbles the figure who has been missing until now.

The queen.

She rushes forward, pushing past the other keening women, falling in the snow, where she lies with her face in her hands, unable to stop the guttural moaning that pours from her mouth.

The Kiss of the Earth

There, in the longhouse, it was decided.

Eirikr looked at his people, and saw the fear and the hope and the mistrust and the doubt and the anger on their faces.

He knew it for what it was.

For three years the crops had failed.

For three years there had been hunger, and famine, and disease.

They had killed many beasts, and two men had been blessed on the stone table too, their blood going after the way of the foals and bulls before them.

It had made no difference.

Still, nothing would grow, nothing but the flower, and there were many who would not touch it, no matter what magic it was reputed to have. So the people had starved, and become weak, and, having become weak, the warriors had fared ill at sea, and had returned not only empty-handed, but short a ship, each time.

So many men lost, so many women left without husbands, so many children dying from the pestilence that creeps into the houses of men when times are hard.

A foal, a man?

A king?

What difference does it make, wondered Eirikr, and yet he knew the laws, for he himself had helped shape them in his long time as king.

And he had lived a long time, that was true.

He owed it to the flower, he believed. He believed that, as did Thorolf, and the others of the cult, and though they all, all the clan, believed in the gods, this flower cult set Eirikr and Thorolf and the others apart.

It was a sacred thing. To drink the magic from the petals of the dragon flower, that still grew abundantly on the western island, despite the fact that all the crops withered – the corn, the apples, even the hay for the cattle.

Now, all the beasts were gone, long slaughtered, and though they had spun out the dried meat, it was finished. Every cow, every bull, every dog, every horse but the king's black stallion.

Eirikr had lived long, drinking the dragon, and yet, despite his years, and his three wives, he had had no children.

There was no one to come after him.

He would leave no one behind, no one except Melle, of course.

He turned his head to where she sat, beside him, on her throne.

She stared into the far black wall of the hall, her eyes seeing nothing.

He looked at her hands, and saw the bones showing white through the skin, so tightly she gripped the arms of her chair. Her lips formed a thin bloodless line, her whole head trembled, the ligaments in her neck stuck out taut.

He knew she did not understand, would never understand, this third young wife.

The first two dead for decades, only with Melle had he ever felt peace, ever felt such joy, ever felt such love, and though she was young, younger than him, now she was maybe too old for children anyway.

It mattered little. He had once believed he would sire a son, but now, he knew there would be a fight to succeed him, a fight between the three strongest of his warriors, and he already knew who would win.

Gunnar.

The wolf.

He had never made any pretence that he wanted anything other than to lead the people, when Eirikr's time was over.

And now that time had come, a little sooner than planned, and Gunnar could not hide his delight. He, despite the suffering that filled them all, every day, strode through the village as though he was already their lord, his black beard jutting in front of him, his hand on his sword as if he was always going into war, something, thought Eirikr with a spit in his mind, that Gunnar had never done.

Yes, Gunnar had been raiding, but raiding near defenceless peasants across the seas was nothing to walking naked into battle.

No matter. It was Gunnar who would be king next, he

could see, for he had already intimidated everyone in the village, warrior and woman alike.

ᛋ

Eirikr stood.

All the talking, all the whispering, all the shouting and the crying were done now.

Eirikr had never been short of words for his people, not before. Not when the crops bloomed under the sun and summer rain, not when the raiding was good, when the children came quickly and grew happily.

He had not been short of words in times of need either, or when a warrior had fallen, or when a battle had been won, at great cost.

And yet now, he thought, as he looked across the silent faces of his people, what words are there?

My time has run.

What can I say to these people now?

I can say nothing to my queen, what then can I say to them?

Their story will go on without me, with Gunnar to take them into whatever future awaits them. And may the gods help them all.

Eirikr looks at his queen for the last time, and from all the thousands of memories of their time together, just one drifts into his mind; an image of them bathing together in the summer, at the south of the island. They used to spend as long as they could underwater, sleek like seals, before rising to the surface, gasping, and laughing.

The image is gone as soon as it arrives.

He lifts his head to his people once more.

They wait for him to speak, and he does.

'Well,' he says, so quietly only those near the front hear, 'so it is.'

The Sacrifice

The first thing to die is that brief silence, before the supreme violence.

It is destroyed by Melle herself, whose body cannot contain the rage and the grief any longer.

She does not care that she is a queen any more.

She only knows that she loves her husband, and cannot bear to see him die.

She tries to stand, and scrambles forward in the snow, but stumbles again immediately. Her legs will not obey her any more, she has lost the strength, and now she tries to pull herself forward through the freezing snow, her green robes sweeping it around her in miniature drifts.

Thorolf nods to two of the women, who step forward and grasp Melle by the arms as she tries to stand again.

She turns her head blindly to each of them, but they will not look at her. Their faces are set firm, and they are strong women, their hands dig into her soft arms like the winter ice grips the harbour, and she succumbs to them, her chest heaving.

Eirikr turns his head towards her. He sees little. He has been smoking stem as well as drinking petals, and his mind is fogged.

His queen, he thinks.

That's all.

His queen.

He does not feel the cold, though it bites his naked skin all over his body at once.

He lifts his head to the moon, the blood moon, and he prays that his death will rescue his people. He is no longer certain that it will, not after the other blessings, whose skulls now hang in the evergreen, but he has said this to no one, for he knows that his people have nothing else now, and that it is only a small shred of belief.

Without it, he knows they will be dead before the next full moon.

He steps from the sled, letting the fox fur fall into the muddy snow at his feet.

In front of him, the stone table waits, a simple flat rectangle, with a stubby stone pillar at each corner, to which to tie less willing sacrifices.

From the top of the table projects a short spout, carved into the stone, thick, and wide, with a deep groove running out from the centre of the bed. It is stained, a deep, rusty colour, and Eirikr understands that in a few moments, it will gleam wet and bright again.

So it is, he thinks.

He looks at Thorolf, whose face is as unreadable as the stone bed itself.

Thorolf nods imperceptibly, and Eirikr steps onto the bed, and stretches his arms wide.

He feels the cold a little now, for the first time, but makes a full turn, taking in the whole scene around him, the last his eyes will ever see.

Slowly, he kneels, then lies on his back, on the table.

Melle's moans become wails, and she begins to tug frantically at the hands that hold her.

Thorolf nods at a warrior, one with a hammer in his hand, who begins to edge through the crowd towards Melle.

Eirikr lies on the table, staring into the night sky, staring at the uncountable stars that are shining brightly down on him.

What lives, he thinks, are lived by the men up there?

What do they do?

What do they believe?

What do they see?

Do they see me?

He wonders about them all, all the many lives that have been, and that will be, and wonders why they are not all the same, why they are what they are. It cannot be, he thinks, that when our life is run, we are done. There must be more to man than that, surely?

That we are not just one, but a multitude.

'Now,' says Thorolf, and he points at the executioner.

The figure in red has been standing statue-still all this time, head bowed under his red hood, knife concealed, tucked up behind his forearm.

Now, he steps forward, and in two paces he's above Eirikr on the stone table, and though he should not, the executioner pulls the red hood from his head, showing himself to the world.

It is Gunnar.

The dog, thinks Eirikr, with sudden fury, he made some trick with the pebbles, with the black pebble, so he could be the one to do it. The dog.

'Well,' Eirikr murmurs, 'his horns appear.'

Melle screams. The warrior with the hammer is by her side, and lifts it to still her noise.

The hammer falls, but Melle, making as if to faint, slumps to one side, pulling the woman on the other side with her. The hammer strikes the woman's shoulder instead of Melle's head, and she collapses.

There is confusion, and Melle slips free, her legs strong again, and scrabbles towards the table.

'Eirikr!' she cries, and now Eirikr turns to her.

His rage at seeing Gunnar, and the cold, and the hot blood inside him all work some power, and his head begins to clear.

'Melle!' he roars, and begins to sit up, 'Melle!'

Thorolf sees that he means to move. He still wields his own, ceremonial hammer of gold, and he brings it down, sharply.

Eirikr sees, and tries to move, but his body is slow, his muscles stiff from the cold, his mind foggy from the dragon, and the hammer catches the side of his head.

He collapses onto the bed once more, on his side, but he is still conscious, though Thorolf has hit a nerve, some part of his brain, and as he tries to stand again now, he finds his arms do not work.

His legs shudder, his arms twitch, but his eyes and ears are open as Melle tumbles in the snow at the side of the table.

'Eirikr!' she cries. 'No!'

But Eirikr knows it is too late.

Gunnar steps forward, and other hands are already grasping Melle's arms again.

Eirikr speaks.

He looks at Thorolf, and at Gunnar, and with the magic of the dragon inside him, he speaks his last words.

'You cannot kill me,' he shouts hoarsely, and yet as loudly as he can. 'You cannot kill me. Do you not know my name? I am Eirikr. The One King! Forever Strong, and though you kill my body today, I will live again! I *will* live!'

He turns to his queen, to Melle, and his voice drops.

'I will live seven lives, Melle, this is only my first.'

The stars shine down on Eirikr, on his twitching body on the cold stone table.

'I will live seven times, and I will look for you in each one. We will always be together.'

Gunnar raises the knife, and the moonlight gleams from its edge.

'I will look for you and love you in each one. Will you follow?'

Suddenly Gunnar sweeps the knife across Eirikr's throat, in a single long arc of silver.

He makes no sound now. There is no air to make the sound. There are only the lips moving on Eirikr's face, but Melle sees what the words are.

'Will you follow?'

Blood gushes from Eirikr's neck, spurting across the ground, making a mockery of the stone spout, spraying Gunnar and Melle alike.

The snow steams, red.

Evocation of the Ancestors

———

The years passed.

Melle disappeared from the sight of the people, no one knew where she had gone, where she took herself that very night that they killed her king.

She did not see the funeral they made for King Eirikr, how they piled the wood high and burned his body and bones on the shore of the western isle.

She did not hear the words that Thorolf spoke, nor Gunnar after him, as they praised the sacrifice of the king.

No one knew where she had gone, nor how she kept herself alive, how she fed herself, nor kept herself warm, and to start with at least, they did not care, for there was still the long winter to get through, with almost nothing to eat. Two less mouths to feed was a blessing.

And yet, as spring returned, and as the grasses and flowers began to grow, and the crops flourished, and fruit hung heavy on the trees, they all came to see that Eirikr's sacrifice had worked its magic, and that he had saved them. And with that thought, they began to wonder about Melle, and wondered at her passing, till they thought her dead, and she had become a figure of story, as in the old tales.

Then, one day, maybe seven years after the blessing of

Eirikr, around midsummer, Melle walked back into the village.

People screamed at first, believing her to be a ghost or a vampire, until they saw that it was a full sunny day.

They spoke to her.

She didn't answer.

They looked at her in wonder. Her green robe, in tatters. She seemed no older than the day she had left, though she was thin, and her hair matted and dirty. Around her neck she wore a necklace. Something she had made, from the bones of hares, and so they understood that she had hunted the winter hare in order to survive.

They asked her questions, a thousand questions.

She spoke to nobody. Not a word.

They gave her a house, at the edge of the village, a small hut, where she lived by herself.

Everyone tried to speak to her.

Thorolf tried.

Even Gunnar tried, but she treated them all the same, looking through them as if they weren't there, as if her eyes saw something else, as if they saw someone else, all the time.

She took the food they offered, the new clothes they made her, but she said not a word.

Every day, in the summer, she would walk to the western isle, and return with a bunch of the dragon, and when she did, people shunned her, for they had come to fear the flower, since they had noticed that those who drank most deeply of the dragon were also those unable to bring forth children. Even Thorolf no longer wore the triple device

253

at his neck, and as the village drank less of the strongest variety of the brew, babies had returned. The sounds of small children once more filled the huts of the island.

§

So, the years passed, one after the other, and, slowly, they all grew older.

Gunnar died before Thorolf, killed on a raid when he fell between two ships, and was crushed. People mourned his passing, for though he had been troublesome as a warrior before he became king, he had not been such a bad ruler.

Something had changed for him, that night, as Eirikr's hot blood washed his face. He had had the old temple pulled down, and declared that there was a new god to believe in, a god he had learned about on a raid to the east, a god who did not hold with sacrifice, or magic.

§

Thorolf died a few years later, of old age, and yet, still Melle lived. People grew old and died around her, until almost everyone who knew the story of her king had died, or forgotten what it was all about.

And every morning, until she was an ancient, crippled and tiny figure, she walked to the western isle and back, until one day, at summer's dusk, she walked to the centre of the island, to where the stone table still sat, where the timber of the temple had long since vanished, and been used to make ships and houses.

Knowing her time was at an end, she lay down on the table.

People gathered round, but she still saw no one but the face in front of her, the face of Eirikr, her king.

She shut her eyes, and as the life sighed gently away from her, she finally answered his question.

'Yes,' she whispered, 'I will follow you.'

And so, their journeys begin.

EPILOGUE

My Spirit is Crying
for Leaving

———

June 2073 – The Flower Moon

Yes, thinks Eric Seven. Our journeys began, lifetimes ago.

I have lived this before, but I will not live it again.

He knows that this is his last life. Somehow, as he lies on the stone table, the moment before the violence of the knife-fall, he knows it all.

The sun shines and the lizards crawl and the clover scents the sea air and the knife gleams and Merle's face hangs over him, blotting out the ever-present sun like an eclipse.

Maybe he *knows* nothing. Maybe it's that he *feels* it all, but whatever is happening to him, he understands that he lived before. He lived other lives, in different times. And why not? It's something he has often wondered about, sitting on the train in the morning, looking from the corner of his eye at the other commuters, wondering why.

Why am I not living that person's life? That man, there, with the sharp suit and the slightly stupid tie? Or that scruffy guy with his headphones? Or that woman, a little pregnant?

Often, as he sat fiddling with OneDegree, he has wondered why *this* life is the one he's had, and not one of the thousands of contacts passing through the device, or one of the countless others that could have been his.

Now he knows. He *has* been others.

A blood sacrifice.

A blessing, so that his blood might bring children back to the island.

Tor nods, and Henrik's hand rises.

Then.

'Wait,' says Merle, quietly.

Henrik hesitates, and Tor turns to Merle.

'What is it, child?'

Merle turns slowly to Tor, smiling.

'Let me do it. I am the child of the island. Let me bring the children back.'

Tor smiles, and nods.

'Yes. Yes, that is the right thing,' he says.

Henrik hands the long ritual knife to Merle.

Eric wriggles in their hands, and yet he does not fight so very hard.

He cannot believe it will end like this.

Merle swings the knife, but not down at Eric, she swings it sideways, and with a stroke, she has slashed the hands holding him down.

With another stroke, she slices at the faces of Tor and Henrik.

The hands tumble away and Merle looks at Eric. Dropping the knife, she shouts.

'Run!'

People rush to help the wounded islanders. For a moment everyone is too stunned to grasp what has happened.

Tor tries to shout. He tries to speak. He tries to tell the others to stop Merle and Eric, but he cannot, for she has sliced his throat, not deeply, but enough to stop him from doing anything but writhing on the table, and now it is *his* blood that washes from the spout.

'There!' shouts Merle, as they scramble down towards the shore, to the rocks. 'I have a boat!'

Eric is shocked too, too shocked to speak, or to question. Merle cries out.

'I knew it was you,' she shouts, triumphantly. 'I *knew* it was you.'

'But you . . .?' Eric cries. 'The tea?'

'Stopped drinking it months ago. Just let them think I still was.'

They round the rocks as the pursuit finally closes in on them, and there is the boat, hidden in a small cove.

But there too are more islanders.

Eric and Merle stop dead.

Between them and the boat are a dozen strong men at least.

They falter, and as they falter, they are seized, with fierce hands and strong words.

They fight, wordlessly, but it is hopeless. Grimly and silently, they are dragged back to the table, where Henrik stands, clutching his face.

Tor lies on the hot summer earth, bleeding into it.

More hands push them roughly to the table.

'No!' screams Merle now, as she sees Henrik lift the

knife from the ground, and approach them, but Eric calls to her.

'Merle! Merle!'

She turns, looking into his eyes.

'Merle. My spirit is crying for leaving.'

She shakes her head, tears flowing freely.

'Merle. Understand. Remember the sea . . .'

She does understand, she senses it too. Her tears and her trembling cease, and calm enters her blood.

She knows that they both believe the same thing, that if a life can be ruined in a single moment, a moment of betrayal, or violence, or ill-luck, then why can a life not also be saved, be worth living, be *made*, by just a few pure moments of perfection?

She shuts her eyes, and dreams of swimming with him.

Immediately, the rest of the world drops away.

The sounds of the angry islanders.

The blue of the sky.

The smell of the sea and the clover.

The knife, descending.

There is nothing now but the two of them, and their love, which has waited for centuries to be made again, and as their blood flows, first from Merle and then from Eric, as their blood mingles on the table and in the soil of Blessed

Island, they are no longer in love, they have become love
itself.

And their journey begins.
    So, it is.

Acknowledgements

For other books I've written, I added an author's note in the back to explain one or two things about the origins of the story. I'm not this time, because there's really not much to say, apart from that you may be interested to know that the painting, as described in the book, is a real painting, that hangs in the National Museet, Stockholm. The original Swedish title of the painting is *Midvinterblot* – midwinter sacrifice.

It's by Carl Larsson, and though the reception that the painting received certainly caused him some emotional pain, the events that occur to Eric Carlsson as depicted in my novel are pure fiction, as are all the other characters.

I would like to take this chance to thank Orion Books. I can honestly say that everyone I have the pleasure of working with at Orion does so with, to me, the wonderful combination of being highly skilled, truly professional, and also extremely good fun. Above all, I would like to thank Fiona Kennedy, my inestimably brilliant editor, because without her, my books would not be what they are. I thought she was good over a decade ago, when we first worked together, now I know I was wrong; she's not just good, but the best.

Marcus Sedgwick
Hadstock
July 2011